Crest Ridge

A.L. Boyd

CONTENTS

ACKNOWLEDGMENTS

This story was originally written for the *Goodreads M/M Romance Group* writing event in 2013. Individual members place a photo and a prompt request for an author to write a story about. This prompt chose me, and I wrote the short story *Crest Ridge Vacation*. This is the expansion of that short story. I'd like to thank my prompt writer Anna B. for writing a prompt that caught my eye. With permission from my prompt writer, I've included the original prompt here:

Dear Author,

See the guy on the right? The one with the tattoo? He's an arrogant prick and I've hated him since high school. The thought of him has given me nightmares ever since he humiliated me in front of our entire Senior class. Ten years later and I can't believe I've run into the douchebag during my mountain vacation. I may be taller than him now, but he still knows how to make me feel small. Will I ever discover why he was so mean to me? Please help!

CHAPTER ONE

"Okay, that's a wrap!" the director called out across the set. "Check with me in two weeks to see if we need to work on any more scenes, but otherwise enjoy your time off."

Rob was so ready for his vacation. He'd been working long hours for weeks on end to finish this movie contract and now it was time for a rest. All he wanted to do was go home and sleep for a while. Then he and Adam could head out to New Mexico. Rob had just purchased a wonderful little ranch in the mountains that he wanted to make his new, permanent residence. Tonight, though, he had one more stop to make before he could follow his plans.

If he didn't hurry up, he would be late getting to the theater for the premiere. Rob grabbed his phone and headed out to his car. Normally, he would have driven himself to and from the studio, but the long, crazy hours had taken their toll. Rob hadn't been able to muster up the energy to drive, so he'd hired Marcus Glover. Marc looked more like a professional model than a chauffeur. Rob hadn't wanted anyone to think he'd become so big that he'd hire a professional driving service, so he'd put in a call to a friend of his at UCLA and found a college student instead. It was only supposed to be for a few weeks, and he'd given Marc permission to drive one of his cars to class as long as he was waiting to pick Rob up when needed.

The premiere of his last movie had been postponed, and now it conflicted with his current work. He needed to make sure they arrived at the theater in time. He didn't want to end up the talk of the town like Lindsay Lohan. When he arrived at the studio's parking lot, he was so tired and rushed that he failed to notice the larger than normal crowd of paparazzi outside the studio gates. He started to get in the car, until Marc said with a nod in that direction, "I think they want to talk to you."

Rob looked over the crowd curiously and said, "Could be about the premier tonight. Adam and I planned to meet up at the theater since he has to fly in from Florida. He should be landing soon."

Marc opened the passenger door to the car for him then shut it behind him after he'd settled into the seat. Once Marc got behind the wheel to leave, he said, "I'm not so sure, Rob, you'd better check in with your agent before we drive off. I think something else is up. The paparazzi have been here all morning looking for you. Tina's driver said they were asking people questions about your relationship with Adam, not about the movie."

Rob remembered that his phone had been off since the director was such a stickler for not messing up the sounds on the set. He turned it on and it exploded in a cacophony of tones for missed calls, texts, and voice mails. He groaned, "What the hell!" as he looked at the first text from his agent Steve.

Call me ASAP

The texts went on.

Where are you?

Call me!

Don't talk to the media until you call me!

ANSWER YOUR DAMN PHONE

Just as he decided to listen to his voice mails, the phone rang.

"Steve, what's going on?"

"Rob, I've been trying to get ahold of you all morning! We have a media crisis on our hands. Adam told me that he's walking down the carpet without you. He's actually going with Chris Barnes."

Rob sighed. He must be exhausted because he didn't understand what all the fuss was about. "Adam and Chris are costarring in that new comedy together. We had planned to arrive separately anyway because he didn't know when his flight would land. What exactly is the big deal with them arriving together since they are officially coworkers?"

Steve's voice rose and Rob had to pull the phone away from his ear a little. "That's what I've been trying to tell you. They aren't arriving as 'coworkers.' They're going as 'lovers,' or 'boyfriends,' or whatever you want to call it. I was going to have an assistant pick him up at the airport, but they arrived earlier and are already at Adam's place getting ready for the evening."

His hands trembled as he struggled to hold the phone to his ear. His thoughts scrambled around in his head as he tried to respond to Steve. When he didn't answer right away, Steve's voice came through the phone. "You still there, man? I'm sorry to tell you like this, but the media is all revved up, and I didn't want you being blindsided. I'll meet you at your house so we can make a plan on how you want to handle the press this evening."

Rob slumped against the seat of the car and sighed. He knew it had been a while since he and Adam had been together. Adam had been away in Florida while Rob stayed in LA to finish his newest movie. As he thought over the past few months, he could see now that Adam had been pushing him away. Their nightly phone calls had slowly dwindled down to occasional ones, and even then, Adam had rushed as if he had somewhere else he needed to be, or someone else he needed to be with. Tears that he'd been holding back started rolling down his face. "I-I… Thanks for telling me, though. I don't know what to say. Look, Steve, maybe I should skip the red carpet entrance and pull up at a side door?"

"No can do, man. You're the star of the show. The producers and investors are all going to be there. I think he's been planning this for a while. I've been fielding calls from the media for most of the morning, so I think he leaked it early just to build up the coverage."

Rob just nodded until he realized that he was still on the phone and Steve couldn't see the gesture. "Okay, but I'm not going to talk to the media about Adam and Chris tonight. I need to figure some things out before I show up."

Despite his personal insecurities, Rob knew his appearance at this event was important for his professional image and he needed to make sure Adam didn't throw him under the bus. He figured that if Adam could change his plus one, then so could Rob. Now all he needed to do was to find a new date. Rob finished the call and turned to his driver. Marc's Native American heritage—from his mother's family—shone brightly. He would look striking at Rob's side. His shimmering, long black hair, dark-brown eyes, and darker skin tone would complement Rob's shorter black hair and lighter olive skin. Even though he was twenty-nine years old, Rob still looked much younger. Marc was about seven years younger, so their age difference wasn't very noticeable. As beautiful as Marc was, he just didn't suit Rob. Sure, Rob would fuck him, given the chance, but they were better suited to being friends. He also knew that Marc wouldn't be offended if Rob asked him on a date, but it was finals week. Marc would probably have to go home and study.

On the off chance that he would know someone who was free for the evening, Rob said, "Apparently I need to find a new date for this evening. My boyfriend went behind my back, and is bringing someone else. You wouldn't happen to have any friends who would like to go see a movie and pretend to date a movie star for the evening?"

Marc's face brightened. "I just happen to be free tonight since I finished my last final this morning. I've always wanted to go to a premiere." Then his face dropped. "Jason won't be too happy about it, though."

"You're still seeing him? I thought you guys broke up a couple weeks back."

"We did, but then he came back and wants to try working things out. Let me call and run it by him first."

"Thanks, Marc, I appreciate it. Let him know that it will only be for tonight and it's not real no matter what the tabloids come up with." Rob didn't want the man getting in trouble with his boyfriend over this fiasco.

Marc drove him home where they met up with Rob's agent. When Marc called his boyfriend, Rob couldn't help overhearing Marc arguing with the man on the other end of the line. "Jason, I'm just helping my boss out. I know you can't go because of your finals, but mine are done." Eventually he hung up and said, "Well I'm going even if he doesn't like it."

Steve arranged for a suit for Marc and their ride for the

evening. Soon they were on their way to the theater. He closed his eyes and flopped his head against the back of the seat. Rob tried to calm his mind and think happy thoughts, but it didn't seem to help. He was exhausted and overwhelmed by the events of the day. First, he'd been dumped spectacularly, and now he'd caused Marc to get into a fight with Jason. He couldn't wait for this night to end.

When the car pulled up in front of the movie theater's entrance, hundreds of flashes from the media cameras bombarded it. There was no way to stop this now; all he could do was try to get through the line and into the building without breaking down. He'd really cared for Adam and had wanted to make their relationship more permanent. Both of them had been busy on their own new movies and they hadn't spent much time together lately, but Rob hadn't been expecting Adam to humiliate him like this. Even though he had Marc willing to play his new boyfriend for the night, Rob's head wasn't into playing games with the press.

Rob kept his head down as he got out of the car, then he turned and offered his hand to help Marc. He put his arm around Marc's waist and whispered in his ear, "Showtime." Marc slid an arm around Rob's waist in return and flashed him a reassuring smile. In unison, they turned and waved to the crowd. As they strolled toward the front entrance, cameras flashed, and reporters called his name asking questions. As much as he wanted to ignore them, he needed to stop and talk to a few of the reporters. He searched the area looking for someone he knew who might not ask about his breakup with Adam. He finally spotted the person he was looking for and headed that way with Marc still by his side. The young lady from *Huffington Post* had always treated him fairly in the past so he felt comfortable talking to her now.

He and Marc paused for photos and waved to the crowds. When asked, he avoided the subject of Adam as nicely as possible. Once they reached the entrance, he breathed a deep sigh of relief. The hardest part was over and now he just might be able to enjoy the movie. He knew that all of this mess would be in the papers in the morning. He couldn't wait to get away to his new house.

Once they got into the seating area, Rob realized that Adam had taken over Rob's assigned seat. Since they had originally been each other's plus one, there wasn't enough room for their respective dates. While they were waiting for new seating arrangements Adam said, "I knew you were fucking the driver. You were paying him enough for his 'services.'"

Rob wanted to kill the man and he didn't care that there was a crowd of witnesses, but before he could speak, Marc spoke up. "Rob's a perfect gentleman. Unlike you and the trash you drug in with you."

He had to stifle a laugh at the expression on Adam's face. Before either could say another word, though, the staff came by and informed them that Adam and his date would have to move. Since Rob was the leading man of the movie, the investors wanted him to sit in the premium spot. Rob couldn't think of any better justice than seeing Adam and Chris escorted off to another row of seating.

After the show, Rob headed back to the car with Marc as quickly as possible. Even though most of the paparazzi were back at the theater waiting for the end of the show, there were a few already waiting outside of Rob's house when they arrived. He thought about the time Marc had told him about his family in New Mexico. Maybe, the young man would like to go home for a visit now that his finals were over. Rob looked over at Marc with a grin and asked, "Hey, how do you feel about a road trip to New Mexico?"

"What do you mean?"

"I have a home outside of Santa Fe, and I'm going there on vacation. I had planned on driving with Adam, but since he's off with his new boyfriend, I'm going alone. I know you and Jason need to work things out, but if you wanted to go home and see your family, this would be the perfect opportunity. If you'll drive my car, I'll pay the costs. When we get there, you can borrow one of my vehicles and go home for a visit until I'm ready to come back to California." If he went back to California. Right now, he didn't feel like returning for a very long time.

"That sounds great. I've been trying to figure out how I was going to pay for a trip home since my mother's been sick."

"Great. Tonight after the car drops us off at my place, you can take my Lexus home and talk it over with Jason. Let's meet tomorrow morning and see what we can work out."

CHAPTER TWO

The knock on his door startled Rob as he dozed on the couch. No one knew he was here. Why was someone knocking? He had bought this house in secret and used it to hide away from his fans and the paparazzi. He'd only told his agent that he would be vacationing in New Mexico without giving any specifics. His vacation had just begun here in his new home away from home. The house sat in the middle of a five-hundred-acre ranch next to a national forest, so it wasn't likely the next-door neighbor was popping by just for a chat.

The knock came again, a little louder this time, followed by, "National Guard here. Anyone home?"

Rob's heart sped up as he stumbled his way to the door and cracked it open. "This is private property. What's the Guard doing here?"

"The Crest Ridge fire is headed this way, and your house is directly in its path. Mandatory evacuations are in place. We are here to inform all residents and escort the evacuees out of the fire zone."

That voice! Rob knew that *voice*. The sergeant major, high school. Crap! Crap! Crap! Just hearing that voice made his heart beat even faster and his palms sweat. Memories of high school humiliations resurfaced from hearing that voice.

Trying to keep calm, Rob replied, "Mandatory evacuation? When did that happen? I just got here this morning, and there weren't any signs or anything on the roads." He opened the door wider and looked out at the Guardsman on his doorstep. Driven by his memories, he started to look up, but dropped his gaze until the muscular man came into his line of sight. Shorter than him now, but the sight of that face transported Rob back to high school and recollections of Sergeant Major Johnson. That dark-brown hair, always cropped short by military school rules, was now slightly longer but remained within military regulations. Those hazel eyes, as sharp and piercing as ever, weren't even looking at Rob, as the man was busy inspecting the exterior of the house. Rob knew he'd had a growth spurt in college, but he couldn't believe he was now taller than his high school tormentor.

They had both been seniors at the same military prep school. The difference was that Johnson had been at the school for all four years, but Rob, then known as Owens, R. K.—as the nametag on his uniform read—was a new transfer-in for his senior year. Technically, he'd been forced to go. Military school wasn't his cup of tea. Being a new cadet, Rob was a Recruit-at-Training, better known as a RAT; Johnson, on the other hand, having been there three years already, was an old cadet.

The insignia on his National Guard uniform displayed the rank of staff sergeant, but he still carried an unmistakable air of authority, even if he no longer held the school rank of sergeant major. "Evacuation orders were posted about an hour ago when the winds changed and drove the fire in this direction. We are here to ensure the safety of the residents. Please prepare to evacuate." Johnson's words jerked Rob back to the present. What was his first name again? Dale? No, Dane? Yeah, Dane, that's what it said in the yearbook. Not that Rob had ever been allowed to use that name. New cadets weren't allowed to fraternize with the old cadets.

A female voice screamed out from behind Johnson, "Oh my God! You're Robert Owens, the actor! What are you doing here? Holy cow!"

At that, Johnson's eyes finally reached Rob's face and narrowed in recognition. "Owens," he snapped. And just like that, Rob felt like he was back in school being bossed around again by Johnson. Sharply, Johnson turned toward the woman and ordered, "Private Briggs, no time for autographs. We have an evacuation to deal with. Go check in with the Evacuation Center. Inform them that we have arrived at our last stop on this route. We will be returning to the staging area for further orders."

She immediately snapped to attention with a quick, "Yes, Sergeant," and hurried off to the vehicle.

Johnson turned back to Rob and said, "Owens… um… good to see you, but really, we need to get moving. I see you've got your place set up in accordance with the Firewise guidelines, and you have a good, defensible space for the firefighters. The winds, though, have been erratic and unpredictable. For your own safety, you need to leave and let the firefighters do their job."

"What about my driver? I sent him out to get groceries and he hasn't come back yet. I'm still packed. It was a long drive, and I fell asleep after I got here."

"Your driver should be at the Evac Center or nearby. He can't get back in here now with the roads shut down anyway. Do you have another vehicle to use?"

"Yes, I have my Lexus there." Rob pointed to the SUV in the driveway. "Marc has the old farm truck."

"Good! Grab your gear and let's get moving," Johnson commanded.

"Yes, sir!" Rob snapped, thrilled when he saw that flash of anger cross Johnson's face as he'd said "sir." Johnson had hated that at school. Rob also hated how even now he felt like a kid when Johnson ordered him around.

Just like back at school, Johnson bristled and tapped his stripes as he said, "Ain't no sir here." Then Johnson and Rob said at the same time, "These are sergeant's stripes, RAT, and you best not forget it."

Rob was actually surprised when Johnson laughed and said, "Man, Owens, just like in high school. I think you always called me 'sir' on purpose to rile me up."

Rob turned to him with a hint of a smile. "Yep, it was fun to watch you get mad."

Rob noticed the expression on Johnson's face slip slightly, less confidence, more uncertainty. "Hey, look, I know we… uh… we didn't get along very well at school, but—" Johnson was cut off from saying more as Private Briggs rushed back to the porch.

"Check-in completed. Dispatch reports that the roads are smoky but passable, Sergeant. We're ready to move out." Just like that, Johnson switched back into his arrogant know-it-all attitude as he snapped out orders.

"Owens, let Briggs here drive your car down. The road can get dicey with all the smoke. You ride with me." Johnson turned and marched off the porch to the waiting vehicle, leaving a stunned Rob and Private Briggs in his wake.

***

Rob sat in the Humvee staring at the smoke as it rolled past his window, but he wasn't thinking about the fire roaring away nearby. He was back in high school. Hazing incidents in military school were sometimes hidden under the guise of "tradition." Rob had been the recipient of several traditional hazing rituals.

The zoom broom had been one. For being caught smoking in the communal latrines, Sgt. Major Johnson had instituted the zoom broom punishment. With his pants pulled down, Johnson ordered Rob to bend over and grab his ankles, bare-assed. Five swats with a broom to his naked backside without falling over was the tradition. Others included saber swats, push-ups, running the box—

"Hey, Owens." Johnson's voice dragged him out of his memories. "Look, I know—"

"We're not in school anymore. You can call me by my first name. Rob or Robert, but stop calling me Owens," he snapped. Every time someone called him by his last name, Rob felt as if he were back at the school he'd hated for so long.

"Sorry, Rob. Um… As I said, I know I was hard on you at school. For a while now, I've thought about trying to contact you. I've wished I could talk to you, to… um… to explain some things. But I don't have time right now with this fire deal. Will you be going back to California, or are you sticking around for a few days until they lift the evacuation?"

"Uh… D-D-Dane?"

Dane nodded. "Yeah. I know you never got to use it, but yep, it's Dane."

"Well, Dane, I was up here on vacation and sort of trying to hide out from the paparazzi, but with all the media attention this fire's going to get, I'd better head out. I don't have anywhere else locally to go. Checking into a hotel would just be asking for more attention."

Dane looked over at him, and uncharacteristically, gently, said, "Yeah, I read about what happened with your boyfriend. Sorry to hear about that. Must suck to be humiliated like that in public."

Rob looked over at Dane now, wondering what was going on. Was Johnson apologizing or setting him up for more humiliation? He replied icily, "Well it's not quite the same as being carried across campus naked for the whole school to see."

Ten years ago, Dane had humiliated him publicly so many times in high school that Rob had lost count. Now he was "sorry" that Rob had been humiliated yet again in public? Rob's ex-boyfriend had dumped him in front of the cameras at a movie premiere and was then photographed the next day on a date with his new flame. Dane, well, he'd done far worse. The zoom broom and saber swats weren't even half-bad since most new cadets were on the receiving end at least once. They were considered an initiation, and mild when compared to the time Dane and the rest of the squad had stripped him naked, taped his hands and feet, and carried him fully exposed across campus before dumping him in the female latrine.

"I-I said I wanted to talk about some things," Dane stammered, "and… that's one of the things I wanted to talk to you about. Please, just… just give me a chance to explain?" They pulled into the main staging area for the evacuation, and Dane found a parking spot. Rob was still trying to find the door handle when Dane's hand on his forearm stopped him. "Here's my business card. It has my personal cell number on it. Please think about what I've said and give me that chance."

Rob grabbed the card and roughly shoved it into his shirt pocket without even looking at it. "No promises, Dane." Dane's actions during high school frequently bothered him, and now Dane managed to cross his path on his vacation, dredging up all those bad memories once again. No, he wouldn't make any promise at all to Dane.

He took his keys from a smiling Pvt. Briggs and headed into the Evacuation Center to find out what he needed to do next. He didn't get very far when Marc ran up to him. "There you are. I was worried when they wouldn't let me back up there to get you. I tried to call, but I think your phone is off. It went straight to voice mail."

He checked his phone and found it had full signal now, but showed the voice mail from Marc.

"That's strange, it's showing a voice mail, but I didn't hear it ring. I wonder if the cell signal up there isn't very good. Anyway, I'm okay, but I think I'll have to go back to California. I know you wanted to stay here with your family for the summer break. I can drive home if you want to stay."

Marc looked around at all the activity and said, "It might be best for you anyway. They're setting up a shelter in there." He pointed to a long building that looked like it used to be a gymnasium. "I'm pretty sure all the local hotels and motels are all full also. The lady I talked to said it might be a week or more before they let people back in. My uncle is pissed because he has to try to find his cattle and move them before the fire reaches his place. He needs me to help round them up so I really can't go right now."

"Okay. I understand. I have the keys to the Lexus. Keep the old truck with you until I get back. Let me know when they lift the evacuation. Be safe up there near that fire."

They said their good-byes and Rob climbed into his car for the long drive back to California. Once he hit the highway, his thoughts drifted back to his high school years.

Rob's parents had never been very affectionate, even before he came out to them in his freshman year. Seeking the attention that he never received for being a well-behaved, straight-A student, Rob eventually told his parents he was gay. He'd told them because he wanted some kind of acknowledgment from them. He'd been willing to do anything to get them to talk to him, even it if was yelling at him. Yelling would have been better than the silence. Being good in school and getting straight A's hadn't worked—nor had telling them he was gay—that was why he'd rebelled and gotten into trouble. Drinking and smoking, joyriding after curfew—things that should have gotten his parents' attention. It didn't. Instead, the local police caught him on one of his nightly outings.

The judge made a deal with his parents—military school

and no record, or juvenile detention and a juvie record. Boom, off to the military school approved by the judge. His parents were friends with the judge, and they figured it would be beneficial for him, and would also "cure his homosexuality." He believed that a big plus for him being away at a boarding school—in another state—was that his parents wouldn't have to look at, or talk to him.

As they put him on the bus to send him off for the year, his father told him, "I don't want to hear from that school. If you get into trouble there, you're on your own. If they kick you out, don't bother coming home."

The abandonment by his family initially hurt Rob so much that he didn't realize until years later that it was the best thing his parents had ever done for him. At the time, he thought that it was the cause for all of the pain and humiliation of his entire senior year. He never went home for school breaks, and his parents never came to any of the school events; not even his graduation. He didn't have an answer for the other cadets when they asked him why he was spending his break at the school-appointed, foster-family home instead of his own.

Even with all the embarrassment, he'd made friends at the school. The most important being Jess. Even though Jess was an old cadet, she was in many of the same classes as Rob, so they were allowed to study together. If anyone ever questioned why the two of them spent most nights in the school library during night study hall, Jess would say, "This is a tutoring session, move along. We need to study." During all that studying, Rob and Jess developed a friendship that was still going strong ten years later.

He pulled himself out of his memories when he realized he was well into Arizona and would soon need to stop for the night. He wouldn't make it all the way back to California today.

CHAPTER THREE

Dane couldn't believe his eyes. Owens, Robert K. That short, scrawny boy was all grown up now. Instead of the shaved head he remembered, the black hair was longer but still respectably short and well styled. Rob had put on muscle and looked fitter than he'd expected—even after he'd seen every one of Rob's movies. The thing that most amazed Dane was how tall Rob had grown. He probably would have to stand on his tiptoes just to look into those golden brown eyes. Dane knew he'd been rough on Rob back in school. He'd had his reasons, and now he was ready to admit them to both himself and to Rob. He needed to apologize—if Rob would let him.

The Humvee door opened, and Private Briggs hopped in. "Hey, Sarge, you know him or something?"

"Yep, we went to school together."

"He went to that military school in Wells? Wow! Did you know he was gay then?"

"No, not then. Not at that school. A judge sent him there. It was that or juvie. He wasn't happy at school." Dane sighed as he remembered Rob's sad face back then. "He doesn't seem much happier these days either. We have work to do now, Private. You want to drive for a while?"

They switched seats and as soon as she hopped into the driver's seat she continued, "Well I think it's great that he's so open about it all especially after the way his parents have treated him."

"What do you mean?" He wanted to hear how she felt about the situation.

She looked at him as if he'd grown a second head or something. Finally, she said, "I guess that means you haven't been following his career, or any of those gossip magazines?"

Dane had, but there was no way he was going to admit that to her so he said, "Nope, don't have a clue what you are talking about."

"According to all the gossip magazines, as soon as he publicly admitted his sexuality, his parents completely disowned him. When asked in an interview how they felt about their son being gay, both of them just stated they didn't have a son. He was dead to them and they no longer acknowledge his existence. Every time he's nominated or wins an award, the media tries to get a comment out of his parents, but they still refuse to accept him."

"That's just crazy. How they can just ignore him like that?" Dane knew it was all true. He had kept up with Rob's life after school and had read all the news about Rob's parents' rejection. That had been one of the reasons he'd kept his own secrets so tightly hidden away.

"I know, but the thing I like best is that he doesn't try to hide it. He's not in the closet like other actors and sports figures. I just wish my cousin had been that open with us. None of us found out about him until after he killed himself."

"Your cousin Tony? The one who hung himself?" He remembered a time when he and Tony had been friends. Tony had hidden his secrets as well as Dane had.

"Yeah. Tony didn't tell anyone anything. He just wrote it all down in a note. I had suspected, but he didn't trust any of us because of our Catholic faith. He thought we would all turn against him. It's a shame, because even his parents were upset that he didn't feel comfortable telling them. They were heartbroken over his death. They'd rather have him back alive and gay than not have him at all." She sniffled a little.

He grabbed the tissue box she kept behind the seat, and handed her a tissue while he considered all this for a moment. "So you don't consider being gay a sin?"

"Well the Bible has a couple little bits that imply that it's a sin, but so is eating pork and crab legs if you read the Old

Testament. Yet people around here couldn't live without their chicharrónes, posole, or the seafood buffets at the casinos."

He laughed at that. "That's true. We'd have a revolt on our hands if we took away everyone's pork."

"Exactly! Even though the Bible says it's a sin, pork is acceptable to the Catholics around here. So I don't see why being gay can't also be acceptable. Most of my family feels the same even more so now that we've lost Tony. My aunt and uncle have started fostering some of the homeless gay kids who were kicked out by their own parents."

Dane worked with Tony's father, Juan Morales, at the sheriff's department. He knew that Juan had taken Tony's death pretty hard, but he didn't realize that the Morales family had been taking in homeless gay kids. Dane looked out the window of the Humvee and watched the smoke from the fire as he pondered over what Briggs said. His mind was as jumbled and dark as the roiling smoke coming from the forest. He had a lot on his mind and he fell silent as Briggs drove.

He thought back to the first time he'd seen Rob. Dane had been picked as the sergeant major in charge of an entire troop of cadets for Recruit-at-Training week. Before school officially started, the training cadre would come back a week early to teach the new cadets about military school life.

Dane was waiting at the Administration Building, to take charge of the new cadets assigned to his troop when he first saw the short, thin boy with long flowing black hair. As soon as they finished with matriculation, the next stop was the barbershop and Dane remembered watching all that long, black hair as it dropped to the floor. All the "Recruits-at-Training," commonly known as RATs had their heads shaved. Only later when they became old cadets would they be allowed to have slightly longer hair. Dane's memories flowed as he thought about the boy Rob used to be. The boy stood out from all the others in the crowd. It was rare to have a student transfer in for their last year of high school. Most of the other RATs were younger, or were starting the junior college program. Dane knew right away that Rob was different. He wasn't at the school because he wanted to be, but he was trying to make the best of it now that he was there.

Dane was startled from his thoughts when Briggs said, "So

tell me about military school."

They spent the rest of their drive talking about the military school. Dane had loved being there away from his strict parents. He was used to a strict, regimented life at home, but it turned out that the military school was in some ways less strict than his parents' rules. He relived some of the happiest moments of his childhood as he talked to Briggs.

While he talked, he tried to push thoughts of Rob to the back of his mind, but he couldn't completely forget the man. They still had people to evacuate and roads to patrol to make sure people didn't try to sneak back into the restricted areas. He needed to get his head in the game so they could get their jobs done.

CHAPTER FOUR

The evacuation orders were lifted two weeks later and Rob rushed back to his new ranch. He had returned to California for the duration of the evacuation, but being back there hadn't helped Rob relax. At least while he was in California, the paparazzi had found a new scandal to follow. Rob's love life was no longer on the front page of every tabloid in town.

Now that the fire had died down, and the smoke cleared from the air, Rob started hiking around to different parts of his new property and the surrounding national forest. The real estate agent and the previous owner had told Rob about all the natural attractions near his new mountain retreat—the cliff face in the forest with occasional waterfalls during the rainy months and the hiking trails through the trees to the north.

Two weeks had passed since his return, and Rob still couldn't get his conversation with Dane out of his mind. Was Dane playing some game? Why would he want to talk now after all that harassment at school? The wondering and worrying made Rob's nightmares come back. Hazing incidents were relived, his loneliness reinforced. *Decide, Rob.* Call Dane; don't call him? Let Dane "explain," or wonder forever?

Looking back, Rob recognized that not all of his interactions with Dane Johnson had been bad. He remembered how, every few weeks, Dane would run his fingers through Rob's hair. It seemed it was almost a caress at times, before Dane would attempt to grab his hair instead. If Dane could hold and pull on his hair, it meant that it was too long, and Dane would say, "Barbershop time, cadet." The times when he couldn't grab a handful of hair, he'd gently pat Rob on the back of the head and give him a "Good job, cadet."

Rob recalled that Dane, in his own way, had shown more affection than Rob's parents had. That was why the hazing incidents had bothered Rob more. Rob had shrugged off being abandoned and ignored by his parents, but to be embarrassed by someone he thought might care a little about him was the worst thing Rob had ever experienced.

Rob decided to call his best friend, Jess. She knew everything. She'd been the one to rescue him from the female latrine that day in school. Even though she was one of the old cadets, she hadn't treated him the same as all the others had. From that day on, she was always there when he needed advice. Without Jess, he might have never made it out of that school.

Rob had set his alarm to wake him up at four a.m. because Jess was stationed overseas in Korea or Okinawa or somewhere like that. Rob could never keep her duty assignments straight. Either way, Rob was going to have to call her at some ungodly hour in order to actually reach her at a decent time. They usually communicated by e-mail when Jess was overseas, but this time Rob couldn't wait for a reply. Besides, it wasn't as if he were getting much sleep because of the nightmares anyway.

Still groggy from the early morning wake up, Rob started dialing the international prefix 011 and then Jess's number. Three times he messed up on a part of the number and had to delete and start over. Finally, after concentrating closely, he got through and her phone rang.

***

"Deputy Johnson," came the dispatcher's call over his radio.

"Johnson here," he responded.

"I know you are about to go off duty, but you are the closest officer we have. Can you do a welfare check at the old Perkins place? We got three 9-1-1 hang-up calls from there."

"Welfare check. Perkins place. Got it. I'm on the way. Johnson out."

***

"Why don't you just call him, Rob? It can't hurt to listen to what he has to say. Maybe he truly is sorry for being a jerk," Jess was saying.

"I don't know, Jess. Maybe it's better if I go back to California and return to work, but I like it here. You have to come for a visit. It's very peaceful here."

"Send me photos. I'm not going to be back stateside for at least another six months, but I'd love to visit then."

"You're welcome anytime, Jess, you know—" Rob started, but stopped at the sound of loud banging on his front door. Groaning, he muttered, "Now what?"

"What's going on?"

"I don't know, Jess, someone's banging on the front door. Hold on while I go check."

"Okay, just don't hang up. We still have some talking to do."

Rob grabbed his robe and struggled into it as he walked through the house, phone still in hand. The knocking on the door was louder this time, followed by, "Sheriff's office." His heart started pounding as he recognized Dane's voice again. What was he doing here this time? It was almost as if the man was stalking him or something. That thought made Rob angry.

Rob yanked the door open and gruffly said, "What now?" without even stopping to look through the peephole to double-check.

"Wow, Owens, is that any way to open a door? Did you even check to make sure I wasn't some crazed stalker fan, or the paparazzi?" Dane said as he looked over the rumpled man in front of him.

"I told you to cut out that Owens crap. My name's Rob. What the hell are you doing here at four thirty in the morning?"

"Well, Rob, I'm one of the county's deputy sheriff officers, and you called 9-1-1 three times this morning. I'm doing a welfare check to find out why."

20

"I didn't—oh shit—hold on." Rob pulled away from the door, leaving Dane on the doorstep, put his phone up to his ear, and said, "Jess, you're not going to believe this."

She was laughing. "It's him, right?"

"Yep, did you hear?"

"Yeah, you screwed up the international prefix and called 9-1-1 on yourself again, right?"

"Yeah, I guess I did."

"Well, put Johnson on the phone. I'll talk to him."

Rob walked back to the door and motioned to Dane to come in. As Dane stepped into the room, Rob handed him the phone. "Jess wants to talk to you."

"Jess?" Dane looked confused as he took the phone. "Hello."

"Johnson, are you picking on Owens again? After all these years, I figured you'd be over that by now. Shame on you!"

"Uh... Who's this?"

"Come on, you don't remember me? I'm Jess. Jessica Jones. Your old squadron commander. Really, Johnson."

"Oh, Jay-Jay! Hi, been a long time. What are you doing now?"

"Stop calling me Jay-Jay, it's always been Jess—except for you. Why are you always so stubborn? And don't you try to change the subject on me, Dane. I told you to quit picking on Rob."

"I'm not picking on him," Dane protested. "He's the one who called 9-1-1 and initiated the welfare check."

Through her laughter, Dane heard her say, "Yeah, he did that the last time he tried to call me. That international code can be tricky sometimes. Just don't go too hard on him."

"I won't. Just needed to do a follow-up on the calls."

"Good. Now be nice to him. He's already upset over you wanting to talk to him. He's worried you'll pull another one of your stunts. Now put Rob back on. I'll say good night and you boys can have that chat."

"Okay, Jess. Bye." Dane handed the phone back to Rob. "She wants to talk to you again."

Rob took the phone back. "Hey, Jess."

"Rob, since he's there now, you might as well listen to

21

what he has to say. No more worrying about the crazy stuff, okay? It's suppertime here, and I've got a hot date. Gotta go. Send me an e-mail after he leaves and let me know how the talk went. Okay? Bye now."

Jess hung up the phone before Rob could agree or even say good-bye back to her. Dane cleared his throat, and Rob realized he was standing in his living room wearing nothing but his boxer briefs and his robe hanging open. Standing in front of him, Dane was staring intently as Rob hastily tried to tie his robe shut again. The expression on Dane's face was a mix of wonder and surprise. *Is he checking me out?*

Rob was blushing as he said, "Um… About those calls. I didn't… I wasn't trying to call 9-1-1. It was an accident. If that's all—"

Dane cut him off. "I understand. Look, I realize it's not the best time, but since I'm here, how about that talk?"

"I guess so. But let me go put something else on and start a pot of coffee."

Dane nodded. "I've got to call this in as a false alarm and sign off duty for the night. Meet you back here in five," he said as he gestured toward the sofa in the living room.

Rob nodded and shuffled off to his bedroom to change while Dane went out to his patrol car to report in. After putting on a fairly clean pair of sweatpants and a T-shirt, Rob went into the kitchen to make coffee. He looked up when he heard the sounds of Dane returning from outside.

Rob's breath hitched when he saw Dane, who had removed his uniform shirt plus his tactical vest and belt. He was standing in Rob's living room in his uniform pants and a sleeveless Under Armour compression T-shirt that clung to every curve of his chiseled frame. A tattoo was visible across the upper part of his left bicep. Rob wanted to reach out and touch that strong chest. Run his hands down those tight abs toward the—*whoa, Rob, remember who you're dealing with here.* Rob was already hard just from looking at that beautiful body, but he needed to get it under control. Instead, he asked, "Hey, how do you take your coffee?"

Dane turned to him with a smile. "Stout and black is just fine with me. I've got a bit of a drive to get home. That ought to keep me awake."

Rob placed the cup of coffee on the kitchen table in front of Dane. "You're a deputy?" he asked as he turned back to get his own cup.

Dane looked confused. "Yeah. Didn't you look at the card I gave you? It's my official business card. My duty with the National Guard is just weekends or declared emergencies. I need a job that pays the bills."

Sheepishly Rob replied, "Sorry, I'm not even sure where that card went. It's probably still in the pocket of that shirt I was wearing. It might be in the laundry, or it might have gone through the wash already."

Dane sighed sadly, shaking his head slightly. "You weren't going to give me that chance?"

"Not at first, but Jess talked me into it. I was going to search for that card later today and work up the nerve to call. But you're here now. Go on, explain it to me."

"Rob, I know I hurt you, embarrassed you, and harassed you. I'm sorry, really sorry. I was actually the one who was embarrassed. Ashamed even. Seeing you in the movies and on the news—how out and open you were—made all those old emotions resurface. Back then, I wasn't prepared to admit that I was gay and attracted to you. Seeing you in person again reinforced those feelings, and made my attraction to you even stronger than before."

Rob had been staring into his coffee cup but snapped his head up at that last comment. "What! You're gay? And—and attracted to me?" Rob couldn't believe it. All that humiliation, all that punishment because Dane liked him. "Seriously—" Rob didn't finish, watching a single tear roll down Dane's face as he shifted back and forth on his feet.

"We were kids. I didn't know how to deal with it then. I couldn't tell anyone that I was gay. Even now, I've never—" Dane shrugged, avoiding Rob's gaze. "For a long time, I was too afraid. My dad would have killed me. The army wouldn't have—well, you know how it was. Things were different then. Even *you* weren't out at that school."

Rob nodded at that comment. "Yeah, well my parents sent me there hoping it would 'cure' me of being gay, but it didn't. They disowned me after it became public knowledge. Told me they never wanted to talk to me again—couldn't be associated with my immorality."

"But you had the guts to come out. I didn't. I'm still not sure if I can go through with it even now. I haven't told anybody— I don't have anyone to talk to about it. I've always felt alone. I guess my defense mechanism has been to push people away by any means necessary."

This arrogant prick was actually covering up being scared? He was afraid to admit he was gay and had liked Rob since high school? His eyes widened and he clenched his teeth. Rob couldn't think of a single response.

Dane noticed his expression and stood. "Look, I realize this is a lot to take in. I just wanted to…" he shook his head and turned away. "It's been a long day for me, and I need to get home. If you ever want to talk, I guess you know where to reach me now." Dane chuckled a little as he continued, "Just don't make it a habit of 'accidentally' dialing 9-1-1, though." Dane dropped another business card on the table. "Just in case you don't find the other one," he added as he walked out the door.

CHAPTER FIVE

Rob had been thinking about Dane ever since his early morning confession. Rob couldn't walk into the kitchen anymore without seeing that toned body and that intriguing tattoo. He'd left the card on the table right where the man had dropped it. Every time Rob thought about tossing it in the trash, he remembered how sad Dane had looked that morning. He wondered if all Dane needed was a friend who understood. He knew the hurt and loneliness rejection by your parents felt. He realized that maybe Dane had been trying to protect himself from that kind of pain.

Rob still hadn't made the hike out to those cliffs the former owner had bragged so much about. He needed some help with the map reading. Military school had provided some training, but not enough for him to be sure about going off on his own. Maybe he could invite Dane on a hike. Test the waters. See if they could become friends.

A week had passed before Rob plucked up the courage to make that call.

"Hello?"

"Hey, Dane, it's Rob."

"Rob. Hi. Didn't expect you to call. Is everything okay?"

"Fine. I called because I need—well I have—you're good at reading maps, right?"

"Yeah, I can read a map. Why?"

"I want to go out to the cliffs everyone tells me are on this property, but I can't figure out how to get there. I can't find Red

Cliffs on the map. Do you know where it's at?"

Dane laughed. "Oh, you'll never find Red Cliffs on the map. That's just what the locals call it. When the water runs over the edge, the mineral deposits leave red streaks on the rocks. On the map, though, it's called Crest Ridge. That fire a few weeks back was named Crest Ridge because it started there by those cliffs. I'm off in an hour if you want me to swing by and show you how to get there."

"Um…" Rob was stuck for words again. This was the reason he hadn't called Dane. Why did he still get tongue-tied around this man? There was silence on the line for a moment as Rob tried to think of something to say.

Dane spoke first. "Hey, Rob. If you want to go out there, I'm a great guide. I've been there hundreds of times. The Perkins family used to let me hike all over that place."

"Oh. Okay. I mean, it would be okay if you came by to show me on the maps. Thanks."

"Great. See you about six? That will give me time to swing by my house after work and change my clothes."

"Sure, six it is. See you then."

Before he hung up, though, he heard Dane one more time. "You still there, Rob?"

"Yes. Did you need something else?"

"Is this a new phone number? I didn't recognize it. The one from your 9-1-1 call was different."

"Oh yeah, this is my cell phone, Sometimes it doesn't work well here at the house so I kept the landline that the Perkins had installed. When I called Jess, I didn't want to run the risk of having the call dropped due to the bad cell coverage so I used the house phone then."

"Oh, I see. Anyway, I need to get busy now. I'll see you later."

***

God this was a stupid idea, Rob thought as he paced the room. He'd grown more nervous over the past couple of hours while waiting for Dane to show up. He considered making something for supper, but he'd only been to the store once since he'd arrived. Cooking for one was generally too much of a hassle, so he didn't usually cook much of anything that didn't come prepackaged. Dane had said he was going to go home first. Maybe he'd eat before he came over. Besides, he was only supposed to show Rob how to get to the cliffs. This wasn't a date or anything like that. Why was Rob nervous about it then? Was it even worth getting better acquainted with the man who used to torment him in school?

Just before six p.m., a train whistle, announcing an incoming text, sounded from Rob's cell phone.

Missed lunch, stopped to pick up pizza. On the way now.

Now he didn't have to worry about the cooking, but that still didn't relieve all his worries. Fifteen minutes later, Dane showed up with a pizza box and a six-pack of cola. "The little deli in town has an awesome pepperoni and green chili pizza. I remembered you like green chiles." Then he gestured to the sodas. "No beer tonight, I'm still on call. Can we eat first? Since I missed lunch, I'm starved, and I don't want to get pizza sauce all over the maps. We can go back over some of the basics while we eat."

"Sure, let's go to the kitchen. I've got the maps all spread out on the dining room table."

The kitchen had a small island with pull-out stools, and as they sat down around it, Dane asked, "What do you remember about map reading?"

"Well, I remember that each little box on the map is one mile long and one mile wide."

"That's a good start. Those boxes are called sections and contain six hundred and forty acres each. Your ranch is almost a section. Do you remember what different terrain features look like when drawn on the map?"

Sheepishly, Rob shook his head. He'd never paid that much attention in the orienteering class because his classmates always helped him.

"Okay, well, the cliff—"

Rob listened quietly as Dane continued to reteach him Map Reading 101. Rob watched that beautiful face light up as Dane talked about the maps. Dane's expression was more relaxed than Rob had ever remembered seeing it at school. It was as if Rob was seeing the real Dane for the first time, and not the severe mask he usually wore.

They finished off the large pizza, and Dane reached out to pick up the empty box. "Hey, I'll finish cleaning up since I brought the mess. Why don't you go look over those maps?"

Rob moved into the dining room and sat down at the table with the maps spread out in front of him. He was so lost in concentration that he never heard Dane walk up behind him. He started a little when Dane ran his fingers through Rob's hair just as he'd done many times before in school. This time, though, there was no grabbing and pulling of hair. Softly, Dane said, "I always liked your hair longer. I liked running my fingers through it, but the school rules had to be followed."

With a sigh, Dane moved his hand to the back of Rob's chair, leaned over his shoulder, and found the location on the topo map needed for Rob's hike to the cliffs. They were so close together that Rob could feel the heat from Dane's body, his arm and shoulder brushing Rob's back while Dane continued describing the trail and terrain.

"Here's the ranch house. This house has been here long enough that it's one of the few man-made features that show up on the topos." Dane moved his finger and pointed again. "Up here is Crest Ridge. By counting the sections, you can see it's about two and a half miles as the crow flies, but the trail is longer." Lightly tapping the map about halfway between the two points, he continued, "You have to skirt this big hill. That adds another half mile to the trip. But you also have to come back. It's a full six miles round-trip. Are you up for that long of a hike?"

Rob nodded. "Yes, I'll be fine. I need to go to town tomorrow for supplies, then I'll head out there the day after."

With a concerned look on his face, Dane said, "Rob, it's not a good idea to be hiking alone. Things happen out there. What will you do if you fall and break your leg? Then there's the issue of the wildlife. Because of the recent fire, the animals are moving into the unburned areas. You could run into something dangerous like a rattlesnake or a mountain lion. I'm on duty until tomorrow afternoon, but after that, I'm off for three days. If you want me to, I could be your guide."

It felt right to have Dane standing so close to him. Rob was starting to think they could be friends. *Maybe more than friends. Oh, come on idiot where did that thought come from? He humiliated you at school.* Stealing a glance over at Dane, he had to admit that the man was gorgeous and not so standoffish since he'd shared his secrets with Rob. He thought spending time with the man was worth the risk and said, "I think I'd like that, Dane. Thanks for coming to help me with the maps."

Before Dane said good-bye, they arranged to meet early on Friday morning. After Rob went to bed, and after what seemed like hours of trying, he fell asleep. The dream about Dane came back. It was no longer a nightmare of teenage Dane humiliating him as he was carried on the embarrassing nude trip across campus. This time it was a good dream about adult Dane and his incredibly toned and sculpted body.

Rob was sitting at his desk in his dorm room at school when Dane walked in and sat on the edge of the desk facing Rob. Dane reached out and ran his hands through Rob's hair. A gentle, caressing touch as Dane let the hair flow through his fingers. "I like the feeling of your hair running through my fingers, but I love being able to do this." Dane then gently grabbed hold and pulled Rob over for a kiss.

Dane was wearing that skin-tight sleeveless T-shirt again, and Rob reached out to trace that tribal design tattoo. Rob pulled Dane closer, until the shorter man could straddle his chair before settling in Rob's lap. Rob ran a hand up to Dane's head to pull him in for another kiss—

Rob woke in the middle of the night, confused and aroused. He tossed and turned the rest of the night, trying to get his muddled thoughts in order.

***

The next morning, Rob drove in to town to pick up his supplies for the hike. First, he headed to the local diner for breakfast, since he didn't have much to eat at the house. Just as he walked in, he saw Dane and an older woman sitting down at a nearby booth. As soon as Dane saw him, the relaxed expression slid from Dane's face.

Rob watched how Dane's face transformed from relaxed to

stone-faced and emotionless in a heartbeat, as Dane waved Rob over to their table.

In a cool manner, Dane said, "Hi, Rob, didn't expect to see you this morning."

"Well, since I needed to get those supplies for our hike, and I don't have much left in the pantry, I decided to try the local fare." Rob noticed Dane's quick wince at the mention of "our hike" before that emotionless mask covered Dane's face again.

"Let me introduce you to the woman you hung up on." Dane said it quickly, as if to change the subject, while gesturing to the heavy-set older woman on the other side of the booth. "My aunt, Elizabeth Johnson, is the 9-1-1 dispatcher who was lucky enough to answer all your 'accidental' calls. Aunty, this is Robert Owens. We went to school together."

"Nice to meet you, Mrs. Johnson," Rob said, as he shook her hand.

"Please call me Liz, dear. It's nice to meet you too. I haven't met any of Dane's friends from school before. Why don't you join us?" She waved at the seat on Dane's side of the booth before she continued. "I heard your new movie is out. Our little small town theater doesn't get the latest releases right away. I might have to drive to Santa Fe to see it."

He smiled at her and then looked over at Dane. He noticed how stiff and uncomfortable Dane was acting. He was about to take his leave when Dane scooted over to the far edge of the booth and patted the empty space. "Might as well join us, Rob. We haven't ordered yet."

All through breakfast, Dane kept his distance and avoided any conversation directly related to their time in school, or how they'd become reacquainted all these years later. Small talk about the weather, local sites, and Rob's job were the main topics of conversation. Rob was again reminded of the aloofness Dane had presented during their high school days. It was as if Dane was two different people. Here now, in the diner, was Public Dane, the arrogant prick who showed little emotion. Last night, however, Rob had a glimpse of Private Dane, the gentle, caring man whom he wanted to know and understand better.

Once he'd finished eating, Rob made his excuses, and left Dane and his aunt still sitting in the booth. As soon as he left the diner to finish his shopping, his train whistle text tone blew.

I'm sorry. I know I was being an asshole again. I need to work on that.

Dane's text left Rob more confused than ever. However, Rob didn't have much time to think about Dane's actions, before his phone rang again. Looking at the caller ID, he saw that it was his agent.

"Hey, Steve."

"Rob, you told me you didn't want to be disturbed on your vacation, but this just couldn't wait."

"Steve, I—"

"Wait, Rob." Steve cut him off. "Just hear me out. I know you wanted a break, and you wanted to stay in New Mexico for a while. This deal I need to tell you about will keep you there. It's for a new TV series, and the film company has a studio in Santa Fe. The director himself already called me to see if you would be available."

"I don't know, Steve. How long will he give me to respond? I'm not sure I'm up for another commitment so soon. I've been waiting for this vacation for a long time and I still need some space."

"I already told him you're on vacation, but he said he needs an answer by next week. It's not that far from where you are so I don't think you would need to move again for the shooting. I'll look into it and let you know."

"Okay, Steve, I'll call you in a couple days, after I make up my mind. Can you e-mail me the script so I can check it out?"

"Already did. Just make sure to call me."

As Rob disconnected the call, he thought about the possibilities of being able to work and stay in the area long enough to get to know Dane better. It just might work out.

CHAPTER SIX

Dane couldn't believe he'd finally met his goal and told Rob everything. Yesterday he'd laid all his cards on the table and walked away because he didn't want to push; he'd just let Rob decide what to do next.

After seeing Rob again, he knew his feelings for Rob were stronger than ever. He needed to make up for the hurt he caused Rob in the past, but he didn't know how, and he had his own issues to deal with. Ever since he'd met Rob in high school, he had never thought about anyone else. At the time, though, he didn't want to be attracted to Rob—or any other guy for that matter—so instead of cultivating a friendship, he pushed Rob away.

There were things about himself that he wanted to change, and he knew there would be many difficulties ahead of him. Apologizing to Rob had been his number one challenge for years. Dane had taken a chance and contacted the Alumni Association to see if they had a record of Rob's current address. They'd told him that it had never been updated, so he'd started gathering the addresses of people he knew had been Rob's friends at school. He didn't want to use the fan mail contact address, because he didn't want his personal mail to Rob read by anyone else. By a stroke of luck, Dane hadn't needed that information after all. He hadn't had to go into "crazy stalker fan" mode either and dig through all those entertainment and tabloid websites. Accidentally running into Rob once during the fire evacuation could be considered a miracle, but then to "accidentally" run into him a second time felt like—fate?

Destiny? Whatever it was, Dane wasn't going to take it for granted.

At least Rob hadn't completely shut him out. He'd called Dane back, asked for help, and accepted Dane's offer to guide him to Crest Ridge. Here at the diner, Rob seemed to sense his discomfort in public and hadn't pressured him. He now believed that Rob might accept him as a friend, and at that moment, a friend was what he needed most. He grabbed his phone and typed out a quick text as soon as Rob left the diner. He watched from the window as Rob also pulled out his phone and looked at it.

"You like him don't you?" his aunt said from across the table. "I mean as more than a friend."

All the color drained from his face as he looked at his aunt with wide eyes. He hadn't expected her or anyone else in his family to understand how he felt. "H-how—what?"

"I figured it out a few years back when you didn't date any girls," Elizabeth said with a smile. "I figured you were hiding it because of your parents. They might not take it very well at first, but I think they will come around. I've been badgering them for a while about their strict beliefs, and I think they are starting to see things in a new light."

Dane just stared at his aunt. He couldn't speak. Hell he could barely breathe. Then she reached across the table and patted his hand. "Don't worry, honey. I won't tell a soul, but if you ever need anyone to talk to, I'm a good listener. There's nothing wrong with what you feel for him. Your parents are the ones who are wrong in their views. Now I've really got to scram and get to work. I don't have three days off like you do. Enjoy your hike."

Dane realized he'd made a tiny bit of progress in letting his secrets out and it hadn't been as bad as he'd imagined it would be. He thought back to his conversations with Pvt. Briggs during their fire assignment. Maybe he would eventually be able to talk to his coworker Juan Morales or even Pvt. Briggs.

***

Morning rolled around more quickly than Dane was ready for. He'd ended up having to work late into the night due to a multicar accident. He wanted to sleep in, but Rob was expecting him and he didn't want to disappoint the man. Worse, he didn't want Rob wandering around alone out in the mountains. He just knew that Rob would be stubborn enough to go on that hike without him.

When he knocked on the front door, he heard a shouted, "Come on in, it's open."

"Rob?" When there was no answer, he followed the sounds and smells into the kitchen where he found Rob scrambling eggs. There were two empty plates on the tiny table and two steaming cups of coffee beside the plates. A stack of toast sat on a plate in the center of the table, flanked by jam and salsa jars. "Good morning. It looks like you've been busy already."

"Morning. Have a seat," Rob said as he flipped the eggs. "Your aunt Liz called. I guess she kept my home number from the other night. She said you'd been up late because of some accident. Is everything okay?"

"It was a five-car pileup with a fatality. You'd think people around here would learn to slow down at night. It all started when the first car swerved to miss hitting the herd of elk in the road, but the guy behind was drunk and didn't hit his brakes. What a mess. Also had to put down two of the elk because of broken legs." He tried to hide his exhaustion as he pulled out the nearest chair and sat down.

"Wow! It was that bad?" Rob divided the eggs up between the two plates and took the skillet back to the stove before coming back to sit down.

"Yeah. I've been up most of the night working." This time he failed to stifle the yawn that had been threatening.

"We don't have to go on this hike today, if you aren't feeling up to it. Eat up then you can use the spare bedroom for a long nap. You look exhausted. You said you had three days off, right?"

"Starting today, yes. I'm free until Monday morning."

"Well why did you even come over if you've been up all night? You could have called just like your aunt did and let me know you wouldn't be here"

"I didn't want you going off alone and maybe getting hurt. You don't know the area well, and with the fire, there could be some dangerous areas in the forest." The real reason was because he just wanted to see Rob after the bad night at work. Even though they were starting to find a common ground, being around Rob just made him feel better.

"I would have waited for you, but now that you are here, finish your breakfast and I'll show you to the guest room so you can take a nap. Since we won't be hiking today, I can make dinner."

After breakfast, Rob led him down the hall and showed him where the guestroom was located. He didn't have a change of clothes with him, as he hadn't expected to stay. He hesitated in the doorway as he felt strange imposing on the man like this. He should just go home to sleep, but since Rob had made him feel welcome, he walked into the room and sat on the edge of the bed.

"Thanks. I guess I shouldn't have come all the way out here like this—" he started.

"It's no problem." Rob said as he stepped toward the doorway. "I'll just go and let you get some rest. If you need anything, I'll probably be in the living room."

Dane watched as the man stepped away and pulled the door shut behind him. He was half-hard just watching Rob walk away, but he was so exhausted that he barely got his shoes off before dozing off fully clothed on top of the covers.

CHAPTER SEVEN

While Dane slept in his guest room, Rob tried to keep his mind on something other than the handsome man in his house. He started by reading a good novel by a local author, but that didn't keep his attention for long. Then he flipped through TV channels for a couple hours trying to find something he'd like to watch, but still his thoughts kept drifting back to Dane. When all of that failed, he found the scripts his agent had sent him and sat down to read them.

He was almost finished with the first script when his cell phone rang. He answered automatically, but after his "hello," he didn't hear anything on the other end of the line. He looked down at the caller ID, but didn't recognize the number. He knew that Steve had given the director both his cell and home phone numbers just in case the signal was poor, but it looked like he had full bars now. He didn't want to hang up if it was the director, but he still couldn't pick up any sounds on the other line. Finally, he said into the phone, "We must have a bad connection. If you can hear me, try my home phone number." He wasn't dumb enough to rattle off his home phone in case it wasn't the director. Now he'd have to wait and see if they called back.

Not long after he ended the call, his text alert whistled. It was from the same number. Rob's heart started to race as he read the text.

I'm watching you.

Followed almost immediately by a second text.

You can't hide from me.

Distracted by the texts, he didn't hear Dane walk down the hall to stand behind him. Dane finally got his attention by whispering in his ear, "What you reading?"

He nearly fell off the couch, his script falling from his lap when he jumped away from the feel of Dane's breath on his ear. His cell phone clattered to the floor and he might have let out a not-so-manly squeak that only fueled his embarrassment. "God, you scared me!"

Dane doubled over in delight. His laugh was music to Rob's ears. He couldn't help joining in. Soon they were both out of breath and holding their sides. When Rob recovered, he found his cell phone and gathered his script back up. He said, "I'm trying to decide if I want to take this job for a TV series to be filmed in and around Santa Fe. I'm reading the pilot script. If I take the job, I'll be able to stay here most of the time instead of having to go on location when we have a movie shoot."

"Oh, so do you think you will stay around for a while?" He didn't miss the excitement that flashed across Dane's face.

"Yes, I like what I'm reading so far. It looks like it will be a decent show." Rob set the papers down on the coffee table and stood. "It's past lunchtime. Are you hungry?" Dane's stomach rumbled in reply and Rob chuckled. "Well that answers my question. Come on I'll make us some lunch."

After lunch, he and Dane sat down in the two big recliners to watch TV. "Can you tell me about your TV series, or is it some big secret?" Dane asked as they took their seats.

Rob laughed. "It's no secret. I'm still reading the scripts, but it looks interesting. It's one of those crime drama shows. I'd be one of the lead detectives. Do you think you could help me out with some of the terminology?"

He noticed Dane hesitate and take a deep breath before answering. "Yeah sure. I could do that if you really need the input."

They discussed the shows and movies they watched and found they had many things in common. Rob enjoyed their time talking as friends. He almost hated to admit it, but he didn't feel uncomfortable with Dane in his house. He'd expected things to be more awkward between them because of their past. Dane's easygoing manner now was so different from the unfriendly boy in school. Then Rob remembered the day at the diner. Dane's flip-flopping personality concerned him, but he considered that it was because Dane wasn't comfortable being out yet.

Dane's stomach rumbled again, and Rob suddenly realized they'd talked the afternoon away. He stood and reached for the empty bottles on the coffee table. "I've got steaks we can throw out on the grill. Let me go warm up the grill. Would you like another beer?"

"No, I'm good for now. I'll come help you." Dane stood and followed him into the kitchen.

Rob grabbed a lighter and walked toward the sliding glass door that opened onto the back patio. "I've got all the fixings for a salad if you want to make one." He pointed the lighter at the refrigerator before stepping out. After lighting the grill, he turned to watch Dane though the glass. He realized that he was developing an attraction to the man who'd once caused him nightmares. As he thought about their past at school, he realized that his fear had never truly been about Dane. His fear had been that he would be sent home to his uncaring parents. Dane had just been the substitute bogeyman in his dreams.

Dane caught Rob looking and he felt his face flush as he slid open the door.

Dane looked around and said, "Where do you keep the dishes? I could set the table and make the salad, if I had 'instruments of destruction.' Shame you don't have a 'den of culinary atrocities' here. I guess the trash can will have to do."

He laughed at Dane's references to their high school chow hall as he pointed toward a cabinet. "The dishes are there. Silverware is in the drawer to the right of the sink." Dane went to work fixing the salad and setting the table while Rob grilled the steaks. He continued to be surprised at how well they worked together.

After dinner, Dane said, "Thanks for letting me crash here this morning. I'd better go home tonight and grab a change of clothes. Do you still want to go on that hike in the morning?"

Before Rob could even think about it, he said, "You don't have to go. I know my jeans are too long, but I have some cargo shorts that should fit you. If you want to stay that is." Heat rushed to his face and he turned his back to Dane as he put the dishes in the sink. He couldn't believe he'd just invited the man of his old nightmares to spend the night.

"Are you sure?" Dane asked. "It's no problem for me to drive home now that I'm not exhausted." Dane walked up beside him and grabbed a dishtowel to start drying the dishes Rob was washing.

Rob glanced over at him and noticed the tattoo on Dane's bicep flex as the man's muscles moved underneath it. He thought back to his dream of tracing that tattoo and resisted the urge to reach out. When Dane cleared his throat, Rob knew he'd missed something. "W-what?" He looked up from Dane's tattoo to find beautiful hazel eyes staring back at him.

"I asked if you were sure it's okay for me to spend the night. I'm not too tired to drive now, but I want to make sure you are comfortable with me staying." Dane set the dry plate on the counter and grabbed the next one to dry.

"Oh right. Yes, I'm sure, or I wouldn't have asked." Rob tried to keep his voice light. With so many emotions swirling in his mind, he wasn't sure he'd pulled it off until Dane smiled at him.

"Great. So what time do we want to start out tomorrow morning?" Just like that, Dane took over, but this time Rob didn't feel any animosity toward the man next to him. Together they finished cleaning up the dinner dishes, then took drinks back to the living room to watch a movie.

CHAPTER EIGHT

The next morning, they woke up early and prepared for the long hike. They started at the open grassy meadow near the house and found the trail into a wooded area with majestic ponderosa pine trees.

"Hey, Rob, I've been meaning to ask you," Dane said as they started down the trail. "How exactly did you come by this place? I know Old Man Perkins hasn't been well these last few years, but this is prime property. It wouldn't have lasted on the open market. Danny Baca on the ranch next to here has been trying to get his hands on this property for years."

"Carl—Mr. Perkins was—still is actually, my godfather. He and Mary never liked how my parents treated me, so when he couldn't run the place anymore, he asked me if I wanted to buy it before he listed it for sale."

"Wow! I never knew that. Did you spend a lot of time here as a kid?"

"No, not much time. My family would come up for visits occasionally, but Dad and Carl started fighting about the time I came out. Dad didn't talk about it, but Carl told me recently that they fought over how my family treated me. Carl tried to get my parents to understand that I'm normal and not the freak they seem to think I am."

Dane watched the sadness cross Rob's face when he talked about his parents' rejection. He didn't know what to say to make him feel better so he changed the subject. They continued talking as they hiked.

When they neared the burn scar from the fire, Dane noticed several areas of disturbed ground. "Rob, I know they had to bring in bulldozers and all that, but shouldn't they have done some kind of rehabilitation on the land when they were done?" He pointed toward the bare dirt and downed trees on the green side of the fire line.

"It's only been a few weeks since the fire, Dane. Maybe they need to wait for the right time to reseed? I honestly don't know. I haven't heard from any of the fire officials since you had me evacuated. You worked on that fire. You would probably know more than I would. If you don't, then do you have a contact person I should talk to?"

"The only reason I worked during the fire was because we were called in to help with the evacuation. You should call the State Department of Forestry on Monday. They're the ones who oversee fires on state and private lands. They might transfer you to the Forest Service, though. I can't remember which agency was in charge of this fire. Either way, one of them will know." Dane scanned the dirt area again. For some reason the area made him feel uneasy.

"Thanks, I'll look into that next week," Rob replied.

As they neared their destination, the pines gave way to a grove of white-trunked aspen that grew near the meandering creek bed. Once they reached the cliffs, Dane saw the look of awe cross Rob's face as he enjoyed the scenery. The rocks of the hundred-foot cliff face displayed uneven patterned streaks of red, black, and white where the water flowed down the side to the pool at the base. Cattails and other water plants lined the edges of the pool. Large multicolored boulders were strewn across the ground under the cliff. Dane had been here many times before, but even that didn't diminish the beauty of the cliff and waterfall.

After a nice lunch in the grass next to the creek, they started back. When they neared the bulldozed area, Dane thought he heard metal clinking, but he couldn't be sure because Rob had just started razzing him about his music preferences. He made a mental note to come back and check on this again when he had more time. His gut was telling him that something wasn't right here.

***

Dane hadn't had such a fun day in years. He couldn't believe that Rob seemed so ready to accept his friendship. Once they arrived back to Rob's house after the hike, he moved toward his truck when Rob said, "Hey, if you're hungry, come on up to the house and I'll make us dinner."

"Sound's great. Let me just get rid of this." He pointed to the pack on his back. Dane took a few minutes to stow his gear in his truck, trying to plan what he wanted to say to Rob. Once he thought he had a plan, he went back to the house.

He wandered back into the house to find Rob already busy putting together a stir-fry. "Do you need any help?"

Rob flashed him a quick smile. "This won't take long to finish, but if you want to set the table again, the plates are in the dishwasher."

After an excellent meal and a cold beer, Dane finally decided to tell Rob what was on his mind. "Rob, I need to talk to you about some things."

"Sure, what's up?"

"I-I don't know how to say this." He blushed. "My-my aunt knows. She said something to me the other day after we all had breakfast together. I'm a little relieved that someone in my family finally knows, but I'm not ready for any kind of 'public outing' if you know what I mean. My parents' views are probably similar to how your parents feel. To be honest, I'm afraid. My job and my family ties could all be at risk."

Rob looked at him and smiled so gently. "I understand, Dane."

"No, Rob, I don't think you do. I've spent a lifetime denying and pushing people away. Hiding a part of myself. I'm an ass in public. I don't know any different. I need you to understand that I won't always be 'nice' when I'm around others. I can try, but sometimes I'm sure I'll slip up. If we are to be friends, please don't hold it against me."

Rob's phone rang making both of them jump. They laughed at the break in the tension. Dane asked, "Do you need to get that?"

Rob just shrugged then said, "No, I'll let the answering

machine get it. I know it's a bit old fashioned, but the cell coverage here isn't all that great. I seem to get texts easily, but the calls tend to fade in and out. I think they need to upgrade the cell towers."

The machine told the caller to leave a message after the beep and Dane watched as all the color drained from Rob's face as a disembodied altered voice left a message.

"*I'm watching you. I saw where you went today. Stay away.*"

Rob jumped up and raced to the machine to stop the voice, but he stumbled as he passed Dane and almost fell into his lap. Dane reached out to steady Rob. The voice hung up before Rob could get straightened out.

"Rob, are you okay? What's going on? That didn't sound good."

Rob's voice was shaky and cracked when he replied, "I don't know. It just started yesterday. When I was reading, and you scared me. I had just received a couple texts that were almost the same as that message. Not too many people have both my home phone and my cell phone, but I don't recognize the number."

"You should report it so that a police case file can be started. We can try and trace the phone number and see if we can stop this."

"I'll take care of it. I need to talk to my agent first and ask who he gave that number to first. It's a new number so not many people should have it right now."

Dane realized that he was still holding on to Rob's waist. He could feel Rob's body trembling under his touch, but he didn't know if it was because of his touch or because of the phone call. Dane stood up still holding on to Rob and said, "Come on. Let's get you seated on the couch. You look like you're going to pass out."

Rob didn't resist. He let Dane wrap an arm around his waist and lead him into the living room. After helping Rob to sit down, he sat in the recliner nearby and watched Rob's face. He didn't look as pale as before and he gradually stopped shaking. Rob was still tense though and it looked like he wouldn't relax anytime soon, so Dane asked, "Do you need me to stay over again tonight? I don't have an extra set of clothes so I might have to borrow some from you again, but I'll stay if you want me to."

Dane watched as Rob let out a breath and started to relax. "If you really don't mind, that would be nice. Thank you."

Dane went to clean up after dinner. When he came back to the living room, Rob had already gone to his room. Dane settled in the guest room for the night. He woke up in the middle of the night to the sounds of Rob pacing in the other room. As he listened, he wondered if he should get up and see if Rob needed anything, but he realized how it might look. He knew Rob had been scared after that phone call, but he didn't know if the man would be happy if he went to check on him at this time of night. He squished a pillow over his head to muffle the noise and eventually fell asleep.

CHAPTER NINE

The early morning sun started to light his room and Rob cursed when he realized he'd forgotten to draw the curtains. He always woke with the sun even though he'd been up half the night because of the dreams. He still dreamed about Dane, but in a good way now. The phone calls he'd received were what kept him awake last night. He'd tried to be quiet as he paced around his room for a while in the middle of the night. He'd tossed and turned all night and he hoped he hadn't kept Dane up as well.

Rob thought back to the hike the day before. The day had passed without incident and he was beginning to see Dane in a different light. When it was just the two of them, Dane was friendly and funny. They liked many of the same movies and books, but they had wildly different tastes in music. Dane loved country while Rob preferred jazz, New Age, and Celtic. They had a lively debate about their own music preferences, but in the end, they both agreed to disagree on the subject.

Pots were banging, and the smell of coffee drifted into his room. It sounded like the man in his thoughts and dreams was making breakfast. After throwing on a pair of sweats, he walked into the kitchen to find Dane hard at work scrambling eggs and frying bacon.

"You didn't have to do that. I could have made breakfast," Rob said as he grabbed a mug out of the cabinet and poured himself a cup of coffee.

"Oh, you're awake. I was going to surprise you. Besides,

you made breakfast the other day for me. Have a seat, though, 'cause it's almost ready"

"I wasn't expecting you to cook for me."

"Well after that shock you had last night with that phone call, I figured you might need it. I'm a light sleeper, and I heard you moving around last night. Did you have trouble sleeping?" Dane smiled at him as he set a plate of bacon and eggs in front of Rob.

Dane's smile warmed Rob and set off butterflies in his stomach. "A little," Rob admitted. "I've had all kinds of things on my mind. I think I'm going to take that TV show job. I'll have to call my agent and will likely have to go see the director in the next day or two. Steve said they wanted an answer right away, so they could start shooting. I won't know what my schedule's going to be like right away, but I'd like to go for another long hike. If you want to tag along, let me know. I had a great weekend. Thanks for everything."

"You're welcome. I had a great time as well. I'd love to do this again. I'll be back on duty tomorrow and I have a few things to do at the house. Just let me know when you want to go. I'll have to check my work schedule, but next weekend is my Guard drill weekend so I can't go then."

Rob almost pouted at the thought that it would be a while before he could see Dane again. He realized that being with Dane all weekend had been fun and relaxing. Dane didn't act like all those star-struck groupies he seemed to attract.

They continued to discuss their schedules over breakfast. Once they were finished, Dane helped clean up and then left. Rob was used to having a quiet home life, but now that Dane had left, it seemed even quieter than normal. Maybe he was getting used to having Dane around.

When Rob dialed Steve's number, he heard, "Hey, Rob, did you decide on the show?" as soon as Steve picked up.

Rob laughed. "Wow, no hello, just straight to business huh?"

"Yes, I told you there was a deadline on this thing. What took you so long anyway?"

"I went for a long hike yesterday."

"Oh? Did you go alone or with a group?"

"Well I had a friend along. Someone I've known since military school."

"An old boyfriend? Or maybe a new one?"

"No, Steve, just a friend. Nothing else. Besides taking the job, I needed to talk to you about something else. I've been getting a few harassing phone calls and texts lately. The weirdest thing is that the calls are coming in on both my cell phone and my landline. Did you give my new phone number out to anyone?"

"I didn't, but I don't know if my secretary Katy might have. She's on maternity leave, and went to visit her parents in Ohio, I think. I don't remember if she gave me her family's number or if I'll have to wait until she comes back to find out. Is it very serious? Do we need to make a police report or anything like that?"

"I'm not sure. My friend is a deputy sheriff and he heard the voice mail on the landline. I haven't filed an official report yet. I'd like to see if we can keep this quiet and try to figure it out ourselves first. I'm not in the mood for another paparazzi scene yet."

"Okay. Look, I've got to call the director and tell him that you're on board. I think they wanted to start shooting by the end of the week. I'll call you back when I hear from Katy."

About half an hour after Rob had called Steve, his phone rang again. It was another number that he didn't recognized, but he answered anyway. This time it was the director and they made plans for Rob to start work.

Over the next few weeks, he and Dane stayed in touch by phone and texts. They never managed to get together because their work schedules ended up conflicting with each other. He also continued to receive the strange and threatening messages. Although he tried to blow off the messages, his heart skipped a beat whenever he heard his phone ring. He wondered if his stalker knew where he lived. Though, he was glad that he hadn't received any threatening letters or packages. Eventually, he stopped looking at any texts from unknown numbers and quit listening to or erasing his cell voice mails. Rob noticed that the calls came from a few different numbers, but he just automatically blocked any unknown numbers from his cell phone. He wasn't home enough to even bother with the house phone. After deleting a batch of unheard messages, he'd just let the voice mails pile up until there wasn't any more room to leave a message. He knew that having unknown callers try and reach him was part of being a celebrity, but he figured that the harasser would quit once they figured out that the messages weren't getting through.

During one of their ever more frequent phone calls, Dane asked, "Are you still getting those calls and texts?"

Trying not to lie, he said, "Not much anymore."

Dane called him on it. "Then why is your voice mail full? I tried calling your cell earlier from my parents' house, and couldn't get you on the cell so I called your house phone, but I couldn't leave you a message because the machine was full."

Rob had to confess. "Yeah, I let it get full on purpose. To keep the caller or callers from getting through and leaving more messages." He tried to turn it into a joke when he said, "Good news is that since they can't get through, I don't have to hear it anymore."

Dane started to protest, but Rob finally said, "Just let it go, Dane. They'll give up eventually."

Dane reluctantly said, "I still think you should report it."

"I know you think it's the right thing to do, but with all the press coverage when Adam dumped me, I just don't want any more publicity. Since I've moved here, the press has left me alone. I actually like being almost invisible for once. If I report this, then it will make the papers, and I can just imagine how big a few phone calls can be blown out of proportion."

"I don't think you are considering the seriousness of the situation, Rob. I'll drop it for now, but please consider reporting it."

Although he didn't want to discuss it, Rob's heart skipped a little beat and he felt a rush of happiness that Dane cared enough to ask about it. Then Dane said something he hadn't expected.

"Rob, since we've been talking for a while, I want you to know I enjoy your company. You remember how I said I wasn't good in public?"

Hesitantly, he said, "Yes." He wondered where Dane was going with this.

"I'd like to see if you might want to go out to dinner and a movie with me? I know I'm not ready to be out, but a couple of guys going out to dinner shouldn't be too hard do you think."

Rob laughed. "Are you asking me out on a date?"

"Yeah, I guess I am," Dane replied sheepishly.

CHAPTER TEN

Dane asked Rob to go with him to a movie. They hadn't seen each other in almost a month now, and he wanted this to be special. They both finally had the same day off. He arranged to pick Rob up at his house, take him out to dinner and a movie in Albuquerque before dropping him off at the hotel in Santa Fe. The steak house he made reservations at was farther away from Rob's place than Santa Fe, but since it was in a bigger city, Dane figured neither one of them would be as easily recognized. Rob was then going to stay the night in Santa Fe to make it easier to get to his scheduled interviews the following day. The fluttering in his stomach grew stronger and his palms were sweating as he approached the door. He quickly rubbed them across his jeans before he knocked on Rob's door. It was officially their first date and he couldn't believe all the anxiety he felt. His heart felt like it was going to beat out of his chest.

When Rob opened the door, Dane's eyes flew wide open and his jaw dropped. He was sure he might be drooling. Oh my god, he's gorgeous. Rob was wearing a gray button-down with black and blue stripes, and a black pair of slacks.

Dane suddenly felt underdressed. He'd put on his best pair of Wranglers, a turquoise and tan southwestern-pattern western shirt, and his favorite pair of boots. Now he felt like a hick beside this gorgeous man who was probably wearing some designer's clothing line. He'd never paid attention to fashion trends. He was happy with his Wranglers and Tony Lamas.

Rob looked him up and down and smiled brightly. "Wow. Looking good, cowboy." That smile helped calm his nerves, now if he could just get through the rest of the evening without making an ass of himself.

On the drive into town, Rob tried to carry on a conversation, but Dane's nerves kept him to short replies. He wasn't used to this kind of interaction. Knowing they would be in a public place with people who might recognize Rob, instantaneously caused his breath to quicken again. His left leg bounced and his fingers tapped the steering wheel as he drove. He had never been on a date with another man before. Although Rob had agreed to his request for no public displays of affection, his gut still roiled at the thought of being seen with another man—a well-known gay man. He couldn't believe that Rob would accept his invitation knowing he still wasn't comfortable being outed.

They arrived at the steak house where Dane had made reservations. The hostess led them to a nice, cozy, out of the way table. Even though they were in a quiet corner, Dane remained tense even after they'd been seated. He noticed people glancing their way and whispering.

Rob tried to soothe him. "Relax, Dane. No one will know. We are just two old buddies having dinner together. Look around. Over to your left is a pair of guys at that small table. No one can tell if those two are gay or straight. Just like no one can tell if we are on a date or not."

"But people are looking this way. They aren't looking at that other couple," Dane said as he scanned the room again as his fingers tapped on the table.

"Yes, I noticed that also. I guess what you haven't been paying attention to is the fact it's mostly women checking you out." Rob chuckled. "Look over my left shoulder. Those ladies are most certainly ogling you. And well they should, because you are stunning tonight."

Dane glanced back to him, and then over to the women at the table. "What?" He really didn't care what the women were doing, as long as Rob kept flirting with him.

"You heard me. It's the women checking you out. Now relax and enjoy the food. I understand you're uncomfortable. Sometimes it takes a while to get over that feeling. I'm expecting any time now to get rushed by a mob of fans who'll want your autograph." His heart flipped when Rob winked at him.

He relaxed slightly and laughed. "Don't you mean yours? I'm not the famous one here."

Rob smiled. "As smoking hot as you look right now, no one is going to know it. They'll all think you're some big movie star and I'm just your tagalong." Oh, he loved it when Rob got all flirty with him. He could have this all the time if he'd just get over his fears.

He looked around again and started to relax a bit more as he saw that people weren't paying them as much attention as he'd originally thought. At some point, he realized that he'd forgotten to pay attention to the other diners in the room as Rob told him stories about the different movies he worked on.

After dinner, they decided to see a new sci-fi movie. When the lights dimmed and the movie started, he reached over and slid his hand into Rob's. Rob looked over at him in surprise, but he didn't comment or make Dane more nervous by leaning in closer. They held hands for most of the movie, but he always held his breath and squeezed Rob's hand when people stood up to move around.

After the movie, they walked the half a block to an ice cream shop and grabbed a treat before heading back to the car. He didn't want this night to end, but Rob had work early in the morning so they had to cut the evening short.

On the hour-long drive back to Santa Fe, they talked about Rob's scheduled interviews for the next day, and made plans to meet up the following evening. He dropped Rob off at a hotel for the night, but didn't want to be seen going in. Rob tried to talk him into going in a side door and up to Rob's room, but Dane wasn't ready to risk being caught sneaking into the man's hotel room.

CHAPTER ELEVEN

Rob was exhausted and ready to go home. He'd been making the rounds all day. He started the first interview on a radio morning show at six a.m. Since then, he'd visited two more radio stations, three TV stations, and was now on his second newspaper interview.

He thought the day had gone well, and he'd only talked about his new show. There hadn't been any questions about his breakup with Adam, or if he was seeing anyone new. When he arrived at his last interview of the day, he wasn't expecting it when the reporter threw several photos at him as she started the interview. "So who's your new boyfriend? He's a hotty. How about telling your fans his name? I'm sure they'd all like to know."

He recognized the background in the photos as the steak house that Dane had taken him to last night. They were laughing at something funny, but there wasn't anything in the photos to indicate a more intimate relationship. The reporter pressed again. "You and your boyfriend there look like you are having a really good time."

Rob couldn't believe how aggressive this lady was, but he couldn't out Dane right now. He knew that Dane wasn't ready for this kind of attention. He needed to think of something fast to protect the man. They hadn't discussed what to say about their relationship even though they were now technically dating. Being seen with a notable out gay man could lead to speculation about

Dane's sexuality as well, if he didn't find a plausible excuse for them to be in public together. "He's my bodyguard," he said quickly.

"Bodyguard? Why do you need a bodyguard?" the reporter questioned.

Oh, shit! Maybe that wasn't plausible enough? "Um—well, I'm-I'm—" Shit. What to say? "I've had an issue with a crazy fan or two lately. It just seemed wise to have someone around to help in case things got worse." Maybe that will work. "It's only temporary."

"Oh! Juicy stuff. Tell me more about these crazy fans!" She looked delighted as if she had a huge exclusive.

Rob tried to think about how to get out of all this and move on. He needed to get home and talk to Dane. Of course, Dane tells him the same thing all the time when he asks questions. "It's an ongoing investigation. I can't talk about the details."

The reported pressed again. "I'm sure your fans would like to hear more about your bodyguard. What's his name? Is he single?" She just kept going until Rob cut her off.

"I'm sorry but I need to get going. I have another appointment," Rob lied as he stood up to leave. He cut the interview short and headed out the door.

The reporter followed him and continued to ask him the same questions that he wouldn't answer. "What's your bodyguard's name? Is he gay like you?"

Rob finally turned around and said, "I'm sorry that we didn't have enough time." He looked at his watch. "The production company set these interviews up and forgot to include the amount of driving time between locations." He pasted on a fake smile and lied. "I'll have my manager contact you later for another interview. I really must get going so I'm not late." He exited the building and headed straight to the car.

"All done for the day, Marc, let's go home," he said as he settled into the backseat. His hands were shaking and his heart was racing from the adrenaline. He needed to get back home and tell Dane what had just happened. He was happy to have Marc driving for him because he was so nervous that he'd get in a wreck if he tried to drive now. He called Dane as they headed home, but the call went straight to voice mail. He didn't leave a message and decided to try back again later. As they drove further away from the city, his adrenaline boost wore off and the exhaustion kicked in. Before he knew it, his head flopped back against the seat and he dozed off. When he woke up, the first thing he saw was a whole lot of brake lights in front of them as the car slowed and drew to a halt.

"Looks like there's an accident up ahead of us," Marc said when he noticed that Rob was awake.

Now that he was awake and it looked like they would be here a while, he pulled out his cell phone to call Dane again. When he dialed, the call wouldn't connect. "Hey, Marc, do you have any bars? I want to make a call, but I don't have a signal."

"Sorry, Rob, this area is a notorious dead zone. With all the rolling hills here, the signal jumps in and out. If we make it to the top of one of the hills, we might be able to get a couple bars, but we are on the downhill side and headed toward the bottom of this hill. I don't think we will have signal for a while." Marc sighed as he looked out at all the trucks and cars backed up on the road.

Damn what was he going to do now? Hopefully this backup wouldn't last long and they would soon be on their way. Five hours later, Rob and Marc hadn't moved. Marc had taken a little walk after a couple hours, and they found out that one semitruck had crossed the median and ran head on into another semi. There was no other way for them to get around the wreck unless they crossed the median and turned around to go back the way they had come. Marc had been considering that option when they started seeing the eastbound lane back up also due to another wreck.

CHAPTER TWELVE

Dane hadn't heard from Rob all day. He knew that Rob had been scheduled for several interviews, but he should have made it back by now. He had to be at work at seven a.m. He wouldn't be able to see Rob for another four days. When he turned on the late news, he saw the report of the large accident that was still causing a backup on the interstate and wondered if Rob was stuck in that mess. It would explain why he was late, and why he hadn't called. Dane knew all about the lack of a cell signal in that area.

When his alarm went off early the next morning, Dane checked his phone to find an overnight text from Rob.

Sorry, tried to call, but no signal. Stuck in the traffic behind that big wreck. Wanted to see you before you started your shift, but I know it's too late now. I need to talk to you. Call me when you can. R

He was curious why Rob would need to talk to him, but he didn't have the time to call. Besides Rob was probably already asleep, so Dane dressed and left for work. He would catch up with him later in the day when he got a break.

As soon as he reported in for his early morning shift, the shift supervisor said, "Johnson, report to Rodriguez's office." *That's a new one.*

He knocked on the open door of his boss's office and said, "You wanted to see me, sir?"

The older man looked up from behind his desk and ordered, "Come in and shut the door."

He did as he was told, and turned to face his boss. His palms felt clammy. He didn't know what he'd done to cause his normally jovial boss to look like a snarling bear.

"What the hell is this all about?" Sheriff Efren Rodriquez growled as he threw a newspaper across the desk in Dane's direction. There on the front page were photos of Rob and Dane on their recent "date" in Albuquerque. There was no evidence in the photos that they were a couple, but the headline caught his eye. "CREST RIDGE DEPUTY MOONLIGHTING AS A BODYGUARD TO THE STARS."

Before Dane could reply Rodriquez continued sharply, "You know our employment policies ban moonlighting unless you have specific permission from HR and from me. Right?"

The muscles in Danes jaw twitched as he clenched his teeth and his hands reflexively closed into fists. He needed to keep calm. They hadn't done anything wrong. He and Rob had only been on a date. He wasn't taking any of Rob's money, but he didn't know why the paper would claim he was Rob's bodyguard. "Sir, it's not what it looks like," he ground out.

"It better not be. I know you haven't requested to take on any external work except for your normal National Guard service weekends. Tell me your side and be quick about it, I've got another appointment shortly."

"He's…" He hesitated because he didn't know what he should tell his boss. He wasn't at all ready to admit that he was gay and that they'd been on a date.

"He's what?" The sheriff's sudden and sharp tone let Dane know he had hesitated too long. He'd have to settle for at least a partial truth.

"He's a friend. We went to school together. We…" —he gestured at the photos—"It was a boys' night out so to speak. A go out and catch up with an old buddy and have a few beers, that kind of thing."

"I see. The article didn't mention any of that. In fact, it quotes your 'buddy' as saying that you are helping protect him from a crazy stalker fan or something like that. Is that true?" His boss's tone had relaxed a little and Dane knew the situation was calming down.

He remembered the strange texts and phone calls that Rob

had been getting lately. The calls especially had bothered Rob quite a bit, but he'd told Dane that he was handling it. He hadn't pushed to see if things had resolved.

"Well, sir, he's been getting some strange phone calls. He told me about them a while back, but I don't think he's reported them. I'm not 'working' outside the county employment policy, but maybe for some reason he's felt the need to try to protect himself? I don't know why else he might say that."

Rodriguez replied, "I understand. However, because of this accusation being so public, I'm going to have to initiate an investigation. As you are aware, this county is gossip central. All of the commissioners will have heard about this article before the end of the day. In fact, one already called me. I have to at least make a show of doing an investigation. We will have to go over all your financials and background checks again, and follow the standard procedure for investigations like this. I'll have to put you on leave as well until the investigation is finished. I believe you, and you'll probably be back on duty in just a few hours, but we need all the facts before I can respond publicly to this accusation."

"Yes, sir." He wasn't relieved to hear this, knowing that an investigation just might out him if he slipped up and got too friendly with Rob. Now he wasn't sure what to do. He wondered if this is what Rob had wanted to talk to him about. He needed to go to Rob's and find out.

In his peripheral vision, he caught a glimpse of his aunt walking by. Then he turned his head to follow her movements as she picked up a copy of the article from the top of her desk. Oh God, she would know. She always knows. Dane's heart started to race and he felt beads of sweat across his forehead.

His head whipped back around to the front when his boss said, "Dane, you're a good deputy. I don't want to see this end up on your record. I just hope your so-called friend isn't taking advantage of your friendship. We'll have to call him in for an interview. I've already sent a deputy out to his house to pick him up. They should be back shortly and if he corroborates your story, I'll talk to the public relations officer to get out a positive spin on this."

Crap! Well that blows driving over to see Rob, or calling him. Even worse, if they bother to check Rob's phone records, they are going to find all the calls between the two of us. Dane's heart felt like it was going to beat out of his chest. He realized he was still clenching his teeth and he tried to relax his jaw as he said, "Yes, sir. When do you want me to check back in?"

"Don't worry, we'll call you when the investigation is complete. You're dismissed; make sure we can contact you if we need to." Rodriguez waved him toward the door.

"Yes, sir," he mumbled one last time as he turned to exit his boss's office. Now all he had to do was try and get his legs to work so he could walk through the squad room and out to his car. His heart was pounding so hard in his ears that he almost didn't hear his aunt call to him as he walked by her desk. He started a little when her hand closed around his arm.

Aunty Liz said quietly, "Dane, honey. Are you all right? I saw this morning's paper. Do you want to talk about it?"

Dane glanced around the room at the other officers who were pretending to be working, but it was obvious that most were trying to eavesdrop. He caught a few curious glances as he looked around the room. When he looked back at her, he just shook his head and whispered, "Not here."

With a knowing look, Liz replied, "I'll get my coat and meet you over at the diner across the street in five minutes."

He slid into a booth next to the window that had a clear view of the front door of his office. He wanted to see when they brought Rob in for "questioning." They couldn't arrest him for anything, as Rob hadn't broken any laws. There wasn't a money trail to follow for Dane's suggested crime of working a second job on his off-hours. He tried to keep his anger in check while he waited. He'd bet that Rob would never have known how much trouble he'd caused Dane right now. Dane couldn't blame Rob, but he could blame himself for having been caught in photos with a well-known gay actor.

He really needed to talk to someone who would understand. Rob would probably know how he was feeling, but he couldn't risk talking to him right now. He didn't have that many friends he could trust. His heart still hammered in his chest while he tried to think of what to do next.

The next thing he knew, Elle was rushing up to him. "Hey, Dane. Saw your photo in the paper this morning. Are you really

Rob Owens's bodyguard?"

Oh god, this is going to be all over town now. He'd have no place to go where people wouldn't comment on it. Stupid small town gossips. "Elle, he's just a friend. We went to school together in Wells. Nothing more."

"So you really do know him?" she asked brightly. "Can you get his autograph for me? Please, hunny?" Could this really be happening? All people wanted was for him to get Rob's autograph for them?

She set up his coffee before sitting down across from him. "So does he have a new boyfriend yet? Maybe you could set him up with my cousin. It would be so cool to have a famous actor in the family." She bounced in excitement as she talked.

He couldn't believe what he was hearing. He didn't want anyone talking about setting Rob up with someone else. The green-headed monster reared its head and overrode his anger at almost being outed. "Look, Elle, sorry to disappoint you, but I'm not going to set Rob up with anyone around here. I think he can find dates on his own. Do you mind putting in my order please? I'd like the huevos rancheros."

"Got it, Dane. Be right back." She stood to leave.

He caught her before she left and continued, "Aunt Liz is meeting me here in a few minutes. I suspect she'll want her usual so might as well add that to the order."

She smiled at him and said, "Got it."

By the time she came back around to his table, Aunt Liz was already there and Elle looked disappointed that she couldn't badger Dane anymore about Rob.

CHAPTER THIRTEEN

The pounding on his front door woke Rob up. He thought back to the first time he'd been woken like this during the fire. The reminder of the fire had his heart speeding up as he got out of bed and threw on the nearest clothes he could find.

He peeked through the peephole this time. Dane's caution about checking was starting to wear off on him. Ever since he'd been getting those creepy phone calls and texts, he thought it was better to be safe than sorry. When he saw a county sheriff's uniform on a man he didn't recognize his heart beat even faster. What if something's happened to Dane? He quickly dismissed the idea as he realized they wouldn't know to come looking for him since Dane still wasn't out.

He opened the door, but left the safety chain in place. "How can I help you, officer?"

"I'm Deputy Morales. Are you Robert Owens?"

"Yes I am. Is there something wrong?"

"No, nothing wrong, I've been asked to see if you are available to come down to the sheriff's office and assist us with an investigation."

"A-about what?" Rob stammered. Surely, this couldn't be about his "stalker" as Rob hadn't reported any of the incidents to any police office in the area.

"I don't have the details, sir. I can drive you in or set up an appointment for you to meet with the sheriff. He's the one who requested I locate you."

Rob was still suspicious, as he didn't know all of the deputies who worked with Dane. He couldn't help but wonder if this man was his stalker disguised as a deputy. He should call Dane and find out. "Um, you said I didn't need to go in right away?"

"That's correct, sir. The sheriff told me that if you needed to be somewhere like for work, I should just set up an appointment. He'd very much like to see you today if at all possible, though."

"Okay, Deputy Morales. I was stuck in that horrible traffic jam out on the interstate most of last night and I've just recently gotten home. You've woken me up and I haven't had my first cup of coffee to get my mind in gear. Do you mind giving me a few minutes to check my schedule and let you know?"

"That will be fine, sir. I'll wait."

"Thanks." Rob hated leaving anyone out on his front porch, but he needed to make sure it was safe before he let the man into his house. As he walked toward his kitchen to turn on his Keurig, he grabbed his phone off the charger and hit the speed dial for Dane's cell.

Dane answered on the first ring with a startled, "Rob, is everything okay?"

"I'm not sure. You tell me. Do you work with a Deputy Morales?"

"Oh so that's who they sent," Dane replied with a relieved sigh. Deputy Morales would understand even if no one else he worked with would.

"Sent? What are you talking about? Do you know what's going on?"

"Have you seen the morning paper? There are photos of us in this morning's paper."

"Photos of us? From where?"

Dane's voice trembled a little as he said, "From the steak house in Albuquerque."

"Oh I think I saw those yesterday at the last newspaper interview I did. The reporter kept asking if you were my boyfriend. I didn't know what to say so I just said you were my bodyguard."

"Yes, well that's the problem. My boss wants to talk to you because now they're investigating me for moonlighting without permission."

"I'm so sorry. I thought by saying that, I could keep them

from digging into 'us.' I didn't plan to get you in trouble. I guess I need to get down there right away and straighten this all out. Tell me what your Deputy Morales looks like so I can make sure the right one showed up here."

Dane described Morales, and Rob verified all the facts: Older man in his midfifties, short and a little pudgy, close-cropped black hair streaked with gray. Dane mentioned that Morales was due to retire next month.

Rob felt much better once he'd made sure that the man on his doorstep was just who he claimed to be.

Rob was concerned when Dane said, "Rob, my aunt Liz is coming this way and I need to say good-bye so I can talk to her. I'll catch up with you later, okay? Maybe I can come by this afternoon?"

Rob knew that Dane was supposed to be on duty today, and he wondered how Dane could take the time off to come see him. He was about to ask what was going on when the line went dead. Damn.

Rob made a quick trip to the bathroom to relieve his aching bladder, then stopped by the kitchen to grab his cup of coffee before he opened the front door and gestured toward the officer. "I'm sorry, sir, Please come in. Would you like a cup of coffee?"

The deputy stepped in saying, "No thank you, I've had my limit for the day. Once my task here is complete, I'll be off shift."

"Oh I see. I hope I'm not holding you up. I-I just had to call a friend of mine, Dane Johnson, to verify. I've been having some trouble lately and I've been a little wary of allowing strangers in my home. I need a quick shower and change of clothes, but if you can wait about ten minutes, I can come with you."

***

On the way down to the station, Deputy Morales said, "I admire your courage, young man. I know how your parents treated you when you came out. I think it's shameful. My-my son he wasn't quite as brave as you were."

Rob noticed the crack in the man's voice when he mentioned his son. "Thank you, Deputy. It wasn't easy, but my parents knew about me long before I came out publicly. I knew what would happen. I don't mean to intrude, but did something happen to your son?"

Morales was quiet for a moment and Rob wondered if he'd overstepped when the man finally replied, "He killed himself." The man hesitated before continuing, "Dane reminds me of him."

"W-what do you mean?" Rob didn't think anyone knew about Dane's sexuality except himself and Liz.

"My son was gay, but he chose to hide the fact from us until he killed himself. He thought we wouldn't accept him because of our religion. I've seen some of the same signs in Dane. In the last couple of months, though, things have changed for him. He seems happier. I don't know for sure if Dane's gay as well, but he had a lot in common with my Tony."

Tony? Rob remembered Dane telling him about a friend of his named Tony who had killed himself. Could this be the same Tony? "What do you mean by 'signs'?"

"Tony withdrew from us. He stopped bringing home friends. He stopped talking about things, like his friends, how his day had been. Dane was also like that, even more after Tony's funeral. They were friends, but I don't think they were very close. I guess I just paid more attention after Tony died. I was worried about Dane, but he's changed in the past few months."

Knowing that he needed to be careful not to out Dane, Rob replied, "I wouldn't know. I haven't really talked to Dane since high school. We just reconnected after the big fire."

***

As soon as they arrived at the county building, Morales told Rob to sit in a waiting area next to the front door. The sheriff called him back to his office about five minutes later.

"Thank you for coming, Mr. Owens. My name is Efren Rodriguez. I don't know if you've seen the newspaper yet, but I've got a situation that I need to deal with here." He held up the newspaper with Rob and Dane's photo, and continued, "Mr. Johnson is a great deputy and I'd hate to lose him over this situation."

Rob snapped his head up. "Lose him?"

"Well yes. If the newspaper claim is true and he's been working after hours, he could be fired, and we would lose an excellent deputy. County employment policy forbids working an extra job without permission."

Rob's face fell. "Oh, I didn't mean to get him in any trouble. It's not what it seems like. I don't pay him. I just wanted them to think I had protection."

Rodriguez sat forward in his chair and leaned his arms against the desk "Them?"

"Oh yeah. The person or people who keep calling me."

"I believe Mr. Johnson mentioned something along those lines. Please continue."

"Well, sir, about a month ago, I started receiving some threatening texts and phone calls. Not just to my cell phone, but also to my unlisted home phone. I hadn't had the home number very long and I'd only given it to my agent. He gave it to the director I'm now working with on the TV show, but not to anyone else. I thought I'd figure out who was calling, but so far I haven't been able to."

"Do you mind if we check your phone?" He held out his hand for Rob to hand over his cell.

Rob realized that he couldn't just hand over the cell phone because there would be all the texts on there that could expose Dane accidentally. "Oh, I'm sorry, sir, but I didn't keep any of the texts or messages that came in on the cell. I blocked the numbers as soon as I received the messages. I haven't received a threatening call on it in a week or so now. But I think there's still a few on the answering machine at the house."

"I see. Tell me about this photo." He tapped the newspaper on his desk. "Do you know where and when it might have been taken?"

"Yes, sir. It was taken two days ago in a steak house in Albuquerque. I had to go to Santa Fe for a bunch of interviews and decided to stay overnight. I had a car waiting to take me around once I got to Santa Fe. Guess they didn't want me getting lost and being late to any of the interviews. But, I wasn't up to driving there in the first place so Dane drove. We went out to eat and watch a movie before he dropped me off at the hotel. I spend most of my time in Santa Fe for work, and I wanted to go someplace different, so we went to Albuquerque."

"How are you acquainted with Dane? You're a hotshot movie star and he's just a deputy in a rural county."

"We originally met when we were at the military school in Wells. But this past summer, I bought the old Perkins place just before the big fire, and Dane came around with the National Guard to kick me out for the evacuation."

"So why didn't you tell all of that to the reporter? That you were just friends from school?"

"Sir, that woman was pushy and trying to get me to say Dane's my boyfriend. Just 'cause I'm gay doesn't mean everyone who hangs out with me is also. To be honest, I was shocked that she had photos of us together. It reminded me of the phone calls and creeped me out a bit. I don't remember anyone taking photos of us that night. So when she showed them to me, I thought of the stalker and wished I had a bodyguard. The first thing that popped out was that Dane's my bodyguard. I didn't tell the reporter his name, where he was from, or even who he worked for. She had to dig all that up on her own."

"It looks like I might be able to spin this the right way. I can cover this as a 'protection' detail and have Deputy Johnson assigned to you for protection while we investigate this stalker issue. We will need access to your phone records, home and cell. Even if you blocked the numbers and deleted the calls, the numbers should still be a part of the phone records. We can try to track them back. Hopefully they aren't from a burner phone."

The sheriff stood and ushered Rob out the door. "I'll have someone drive you home shortly, and they can pick up the recordings on your home phone. I'll need you to sign a waiver to access your cell records also. We'll track this down. You really should have come in earlier to do a report, though."

Rodriguez left Rob back in the waiting room, and went back toward his office gesturing to another deputy on duty to follow.

CHAPTER FOURTEEN

Dane looked down at his watch then back out the window. It had been almost an hour since Rob had walked in the door, but he hadn't come back out yet. He'd eaten breakfast and had more cups of coffee then he could count. Now he just stared out the window and shredded his napkin. Elle came around occasionally asking if he needed anything else. He was relieved when she hadn't tried to bother him again about Rob's autograph or setting up that date with her cousin. Even though he'd finished his breakfast a while ago, he didn't order anything else, but he knew they wouldn't kick out. Even though the owner often gave away free coffee to the deputies, Dane always made sure to pay his bills and tip the waitresses well when he visited.

Aunt Liz had already gone back to work. Before she left, she told him, "You might be able to keep this quiet for now, but do you want to keep hiding for the rest of your life? I'll support you no matter what you decide to do, hun. They can't kick you out of the Guard anymore, and if they give you too much trouble over at the sheriff's office, they'll have to deal with me and Juan."

His heart skipped a beat when he heard that. "Juan? He knows?"

"I don't know if he knows for sure, but he came to me a few months back when you were looking so down. He was worried that you might do something like Tony. I've never told him anything, but after all that he's dealt with—let's just say he's a very supportive man. You need to talk this over with Rob. Don't make a rash decision without talking to him about it."

After she left, he mulled over what she'd said. He still didn't think he was ready for being fully open about his sexuality, but he knew it would come out eventually because of Rob's high-profile life. He and Rob needed to have a long talk though before he made that choice.

Just then, his phone buzzed. It was his boss already. "Johnson."

"If you haven't gone too far away, better get back over here. I've got a job for you."

He couldn't hold back the smile. "Yes, sir, I'm just across the street at the diner."

When he walked back to the office, he looked through the window on the door and saw Aunt Liz sitting next to Rob holding his hand. He couldn't hear what they were saying, but they both looked up when he opened the door. Liz patted Rob's hand and stood. "I'll let you boys talk."

He flashed Rob a hesitant smile and said, "Sorry, but I've got to go meet up with my boss for a minute. I'll be right back." Then he turned, and walked toward the sheriff's office.

Rodriguez must have seen him coming because he was waiting at the door. As soon as Dane crossed the threshold, Rodriguez closed the door and immediately started. "Dane, we've done a quick review and haven't found anything out of the ordinary. Your buddy out there has confirmed that he has a bit of a stalker problem, and we're going to go ahead and reinstate you to duty. I'll have the public relations office release a statement that you were officially assigned to Mr. Owens on protection duty during the time that photo was taken. Apparently, the reporter didn't know that you and Mr. Owens are friends. I'm hoping that we can avoid any perception of favoritism. Make sure we don't have any issues like personal feelings and friendships getting in the way of the case, because we are officially opening an investigation on the stalker now that Mr. Owens has reported it. He's agreed to give us access to his home phone records. We need to get copies of his voice mails from his home answering machine. We will also need to check his texts and cell phone records. Take him home and call in the State Police Crime Scene Team to help you. We don't have the resources to do in-depth phone checks. Also, if the calls are coming from out of the county or state, they will have better luck coordinating with other resources to do the follow-up." The sheriff looked down at a file on his desk.

"I understand, sir." Dane paused to see if his boss had more to say to him. When he didn't look up from his reading, Dane finally said, "Will that be all, sir?"

"Yes, that will be all." Dane headed for the door, but just as he reached for the handle, the sheriff said, "If you have something on your mind, my door is always open."

Dane looked back at the man and hesitated. "Thank you, sir. I'll keep that in mind."

Dane found Rob still sitting in the waiting room. "Looks like I'm taking you home. I need to call in the state investigators and have them meet us at your house to get the recordings off your home phone. Give me a couple more minutes, and then we can go."

His gut clenched as he made the necessary calls while trying to avoid the glances from his coworkers. He hadn't heard the rumors that were floating around, but the way people were whispering and staring, he knew something was being said. Damned small town gossip. He needed to get out of here before he blew a gasket.

CHAPTER FIFTEEN

As soon as they got in Dane's car, Rob started. "Dane, look I'm sorry I got you in trouble. I didn't realize how big of a deal that would be." He knew that Dane was worried about being outed, but he hoped he'd been able to avoid that due to the circumstances. Then he remembered their phone calls and recent texts just as Dane started speaking.

"It worked out okay, Rob, don't worry about it. But—" Dane's hands gripped the steering wheel so tightly it looked like he'd break it.

"Yeah I know." Rob interrupted, "I've got to do something about all these texts on here from you." He held up his cell phone and waved it in front of himself as he spoke. "Your boss asked to see it for the stalker message, but I told him I'd deleted those already. He didn't make me hand the phone over, so you're safe on that for now. Your number will show up on my phone records, but if I delete all these texts, will they show up also?"

Dane's hands relaxed a little on the steering wheel as he spoke. "The Crime Scene Team can usually recover most anything, but they shouldn't be worried about calls and texts from the people you know. They should be digging into the calls from unknown numbers. There is still a chance though that they will recover and find our texts. I think you should leave it alone for now. If it outs me, I think I can handle it."

Rob could see beads of sweat forming on Dane's forehead, and the rigid set of his muscles. Rob could tell that Dane was lying, but he didn't say anything else. He didn't want to push Dane into anything. Silence fell between them as they continued the drive home. Rob knew Dane was still worrying about being caught.

Although Dane said he could handle being outed, as soon as they arrived back at Rob's house he started pacing the living room. Rob tried to get him to settle down and have a drink or watch a movie, but he only sat still for a few moments before he started fidgeting, then he'd stand and go back to pacing.

When they were alone together, or from their times talking on the phone, Rob had never seen Dane this agitated before. He realized that he'd caused this trouble for Dane, but the man didn't seem mad at him. Rob spoke up. "Dane, shouldn't we talk about what we will say when the team gets here? I don't want to mess up again and say the wrong things."

Dane ran his fingers thorough his hair as he stopped his pacing. Then he took several deep breaths before he spoke, "You didn't mess things up, Rob. I knew this would happen eventually, but I just wasn't expecting it to happen so soon."

"I understand, Dane—" Rob snapped his mouth shut as they heard the rumble of a motor as a vehicle came to a stop outside. Dane went to the door and looked through the peephole before opening the door. Rob heard Dane sigh and watched as the tense muscles in his back and shoulders began to relax. He heard Dane mutter something under his breath.

"Everything okay, Dane? Is it someone you know?" He was happy to see the man finally starting to relax if only just a little.

Dane looked over his shoulder and flashed Rob a quick smile. "Do you remember Private Briggs from the day of the evacuation?"

He vaguely remembered the woman who'd yelled at him. "Was she the loud one who wanted my autograph?" He'd been so focused on seeing Dane again that he'd mostly blanked out the rest of the crew who had been with the man.

"Yes, that's her. She's a part of the state investigators unit. Her uncle is Deputy Morales, the man who brought you in. I think she'll be careful with the information. I don't get to choose which investigators the state sends over, but I'm happy they sent her team."

They heard the team stepping up onto the porch just then, and Dane opened the door to invite them into Rob's living room.

Angela Briggs stepped in followed by two other investigators. "Hi, Dane." She shook his hand then walked over to Rob and stuck out her hand. "Mr. Owens, it's good to see you again." She blushed as she continued, "I know I sounded like a teenage girl the last time we met, but I was excited to see one of my favorite actors. I'm a big fan of yours. As soon as I saw the request for assistance here, I wanted to meet you again. Apparently, it's not on much better terms is it?"

Rob laughed. "No, not really."

"Well, come sit down and tell me what's been going on and we will see what we can do to help. Dane will you brief them on the case please." She waved over to her companions before sitting down beside Rob on the couch.

CHAPTER SIXTEEN

Dane went over to the others on the team and briefed them on Rob's stalker. He positioned himself so that he could watch as Rob explained the situation with the harassing phone calls and texts. Even with all the other people in the room, he couldn't keep his eyes off Rob. He saw Rob motion to his answering machine in the other room as he told her that it was full of messages. Dane knew Rob hadn't bothered to listen to many of the messages on his machine. He hadn't realized that Rob been telling people to leave a message on his cell or text him if he didn't answer because he didn't want to bother going through all the hateful messages on the answering machine. Dane just wished he'd known how bad it really was, but Rob had mostly kept quiet on the topic.

Angela called out, "Hey, Keith, check out the answering machine and make a copy of all the messages on there. Dane, you got a minute?" She waved him over.

"What's up, Angela?" he asked as he sat down in the chair and glanced over at Rob. "Everything okay?"

"I have Rob's statement, but I wanted to check with you and see if there was anything else that I've missed?"

Dane looked over at Rob. When he caught sight of Rob's quick smile and slight nod, he knew it was time. He looked back at Angela and said, "You are going to find a large number of calls between Rob and my cell number. I'm aware that you will be looking into the stalker calls, but it might come up. If you pull his complete call and text history, there will be things in the record that are personal between Rob and—" He looked over at Rob again to draw on his courage. Taking a deep breath he continued, "We're dating, but I'm not out yet. You're the second person I've told. I need to know though if those texts will be a part of the investigation."

Angela's eyes went wide as she stared at the two of them. She smiled widely as she turned to Rob and said, "Give me a list of all the phone numbers you consider 'safe' including Dane's and we will try to only focus on the unknown numbers." Looking back at him she continued, "I think we can work around this."

He smiled at her. "Thanks, Angela. I really appreciate this." He felt a wave of relief knowing that his secret was safe a while longer. He trusted Angela to keep that information to herself.

He watched as Rob worked on his safe list. "Rob, you'd better indicate on your list which people on your safe list have both your home and cell numbers. You said that the house line was new and only a few people have that one."

Before Rob could respond, his home phone rang.

Angela said, "We have the phone monitored now, and can trace the call if we need to."

Rob went over and looked at the caller ID. "No need, it's just my agent calling. I'll need to take this."

Dane heard him say, "Hello, Steve."

He watched Rob grimace at whatever his agent said. Then Rob responded, "Well not really. It's about that issue I called you about a while back, the harassing phone calls and stuff. I can't say too much right now, but the police are investigating. Let me call you back in a few hours after they've finished whatever they need to do here."

Angela poked Dane in the side. "Don't stare too hard. Your eyeballs might fall out," she said with a smile. "He's cute. If he wasn't gay, I'd be chasing after him myself." She laughed when he glared at her. "Don't worry. We'll get this problem worked out." Dane knew she was talking about more than just Rob's stalker problem. She was going to help protect his secret as well.

After Rob hung up the phone, Angela looked over his list and asked about each individual. Besides Dane, there was his agent Steve, his current director Jon, his driver Marc, and a few close friends.

Dane looked at Angela and said, "We can rule out Jess for sure. She's stationed overseas in the Army and it's highly unlikely she'd ruin her career on something stupid like this. The Perkins are Rob's godparents, so I wouldn't put them at the top of the suspect list either. Marc looks like the wild card here, and I think we'll need to consider him in the suspect pool." He looked over at Rob. "The calls didn't start until you moved here right, Rob?"

Rob nodded. "Yeah, I'd been here a little over a month before I got the first call. I've been ignoring them for about another month. Why?"

"Marc has known your phone numbers and where you live this whole time?" he asked.

"Yes. I've known Marc for a while now. I hired him to drive me around on my last movie. He has all of my phone numbers, just in case. His family lives in the area, and he said he wanted to come back to see them over his college summer break. He's due to go back to school shortly. I don't really need him to drive me back and forth to the set, but I figured he could do with an easy summer job while he's in the area."

Angela said, "Who is the guy you took to your last premiere when Adam left you for another guy? Could he be your stalker?"

Rob smiled. "That was Marc. He filled in at the last minute. He had a boyfriend then, Jason—" Frustration crossed his face as Rob struggled to remember. "I can't remember his last name. Anyway, later Marc told me that Jason got mad about that night when Marc was splashed all over the news hanging on me like a new lover. It was all just an act and Jason knew in advance, but it apparently made Jason jealous."

"Jealous enough to stalk you?" Dane and Angela asked at the same time.

Rob shrugged. "Honestly, I don't know. Marc never said, but I don't think that Marc would have given him my phone numbers. Unless he secretly went through Marc's phone, I don't know how else he would have had access to my phone numbers."

"We still need to check this Jason out," Dane said as he made a note on Rob's list.

CHAPTER SEVENTEEN

After Angela and her team left, Dane said, "Well looks like you are stuck with me for a while. Do you need to go anywhere today?" He hoped that he and Rob would finally have some private time together. Other than the phone calls and the one date, they hadn't had a chance to be together since their hike a month ago.

"No, not today. I go back to work tomorrow. The director gave me today off 'to recover' from all those interviews this weekend." Rob gave him a wicked smile. "Are you coming to work with me tomorrow?"

He smiled. "I don't know how much recovering you are going to do today if you keep giving me looks like that. As for tomorrow, I'll need to call the boss and see if he wants me to go with you on your days at work, but I'm not sure since we have to cross the county line. They may have to set up a state police protection detail."

"It would be cool if you could come and see what I do, but I understand if you can't. That was amazing how you came out to Angela."

"I'm glad that Angela took the news so well, but I don't think I can tell everyone just yet."

Rob walked over to him and pulled him in for a hug. "I know that was difficult, but I'm glad you did it."

"It was easier than I thought, but I knew Angela would understand. It was her cousin, Tony, I told you about. She and I talked about his suicide that day after we dropped you off at the Evac Center." He pulled back from Rob's hug and looked him over. The long day yesterday and the early morning wakeup call were starting to take their toll on Rob.

Dane looked toward Rob's bedroom and said, "You look tired. I know it was a rough night last night. Do you want to go back to bed?" As much as he wanted to spend time with Rob, it wouldn't be any good if Rob passed out from fatigue.

"Only if you come with me. I want to spend more time with you. It's crazy how we haven't been able to coordinate a schedule that works for both of us." Rob's lips barely turned up and Dane could see the fatigue all over his face.

"I'll be right in. Let me lock up first." He figured if he took his time, Rob would be asleep by the time he got to the bedroom. It was obvious that the long day yesterday had sapped Rob's energy.

As he'd predicted, Rob was fast asleep on top of the covers dressed in only his boxers. Dane also stripped down to his briefs, crawled in the bed with him, and spooned up behind him. He laid his forehead against the back of Rob's neck and lightly kissed him between the shoulder blades.

He marveled at Rob's smooth skin. He'd known that Rob had inherited his dark hair and olive skin from his Italian mother. Dane had seen photos of Rob's parents over the years. Rob had kept one with him at school, and they occasionally made it into the papers when reporters tried to interview them.

He could easily stroke his hand down Rob's smooth chest and abs to his cock, but he wanted Rob to sleep a while before they played. He hadn't seen Rob undressed since high school when he'd ordered his squad to carry the boy to the girls' latrine. Dane had stayed back on purpose claiming he needed to keep an eye out for the cadets on Guard duty, but really, he'd wanted to ogle Rob's body.

In the past, Dane had kept his encounters with other men to a minimum. He was used to hasty blowjobs in back alleys and restroom stalls. Being here with Rob, almost naked and in a bed, was a completely new experience. He wanted to make it last. He thought he wasn't tired, but he soon drifted off to sleep.

When Dane woke up, he was now the inside spoon, with Rob wrapped around him. Rob's hard erection was poking him in the back. He was using one of Rob's arms as a pillow and the other trailed down his chest as it headed for his already hard cock. He moaned as the hand stopped in the patch of hair just above his briefs. He lifted his hips to entice Rob to go farther.

Rob whispered in his ear, "Looks like you're finally awake."

Dane turned his head and looked into Rob's eyes. "Me? You were the one passed out when I came back from locking up. Guess I'm not the only sleepyhead." He searched out Rob's lips and kissed him. Rob's lips parted and he deepened the kiss. When they finally parted, he leaned into Rob as he tried to catch his breath.

Rob smiled back. "True, but we're awake now. I wanted you inside me, but I've screwed up." He ducked his head as a blush crept across his face. "With all that's happened in the last few days, I forgot the condoms."

Dane rolled over and kissed him gently. "That's okay. We can still do other things." He reached down and rubbed Rob's shaft through the cotton material. "But first, we need to get rid of these." He gently pushed Rob onto his back.

Dane couldn't believe how beautiful Rob looked: dark hair tousled from sleep and the light stubble on his cheeks. Dane couldn't resist kissing him again. He gently rubbed his hands over Rob's well-defined chest. Over those dark nubs. He slowly slid down Rob's body, trailing kisses as he went. When he reached his groin, he pulled Rob's boxers down and finally got a good look at his cock. After slinging Rob's boxers across the room, he removed his own before kneeling between Rob's parted legs.

He leaned over Rob's chest and licked one of Rob's nipples. Their cocks brushed together as he sucked the nub into his mouth while he flicked his thumb over the other one. Rob moaned and writhed under him as he continued to play.

After a few moments, he slowly worked his way back down Rob's body, kissing as he went. When he reached Rob's cock, he wrapped one hand around it. The cock twitched in his hand as he looked down and enjoyed the view. Finally, he leaned in and licked the crown. Rob's hips bucked up as Dane drew back and blew on the moistened head.

Rob groaned. "Tease."

Dane looked up and saw a smile cross Rob's beautiful face. With Rob's dick still in one hand, he reached down and rolled Rob's balls around with his other hand. Then he went back to work. He kept one hand stroking Rob's cock while the other hand wandered up and over Rob's chest. He played with Rob's nipples as he sucked.

He felt Rob's hand running first through his short hair then over his back and shoulders. After a few short minutes, Rob tapped him on his head and said, "Turn around. I want to taste you too." A huge smile crossed Dane's face as he looked up at Rob.

Dane shuffled around and straddled Rob's head before dipping down to suck Rob's cock back into this mouth. He moaned when Rob's mouth closed around his own dick and felt a sensation start in his belly. He knew he wouldn't last long. It had been a while since he'd been with anyone.

He continued to work Rob's cock with his tongue. Slipping up and down his shaft and swirling his tongue around the head. He held himself up with one hand while he ran the other hand up and down Rob's shaft in sync with his mouth.

He felt Rob's hand caress his balls and then move up over his thigh to message his ass. He soon felt Rob stiffen and Dane's cock dropped from Rob's mouth. Rob moaned huskily, "Close, Dane."

Shortly thereafter, Rob's hot cum was pulsing into his mouth. He could feel Rob's hot breath panting against his cock as Rob released. Rob then took him back into his mouth, and Dane didn't last long.

Dane could barely move after such an explosive orgasm, but he managed to twist around and snuggle into Rob's side. He loved hearing Rob call his name as he'd come. He wanted more of all this. More of Rob curled up around him. More wonderful times like this. His mind wandered, as they lay there cuddled together until they both fell asleep.

It was afternoon before they got up, made lunch, and moved to the couch for the afternoon. They snuggled on the couch to watch TV, but ended up making out like a pair of horny teenagers all afternoon. Later, Dane helped Rob prepare dinner. He enjoyed watching Rob in the kitchen and was acutely aware of how domestic the scene was. He hadn't had this kind of experience before, and now he realized how much he'd missed by not being open to his friends and family.

After dinner, when he and Rob were settled back on the couch for the evening, he said, "Rob, we need to talk about a few things."

Rob stiffened beside him as he said, "Dane, I really am sorry—"

Dane interrupted, "No it's not what you are thinking. I want to be more open to my family and friends, but I'm still not ready to go totally public as your boyfriend… If that's really where this is headed." He gestured between himself and Rob. "For a while, I think we can still use the excuse that I'm your bodyguard. I'd like us to go out on another date, but until this stalker thing is handled, it will be difficult. After that, I don't know what you want your manager to tell the press. Do you have any suggestions?"

Rob gently kissed him. "I think we can just tell the truth." Before Dane could protest, Rob continued. "We went to school together. That's true enough. If they check the school records, they'll be able to verify it anyway. We just say we went to school together, but lost touch after graduation. When this stalker issue came up, we reconnected and started hanging out as buddies. Then when or if you want to come out publicly, I hope it would be less of a big deal. How does that work for you?"

Dane smiled at him. He was happy that Rob understood his fears and helped him see the good things he'd been missing all these years. "That sounds perfect to me. We can still go places together. Have date nights and not look like we are on a date."

Rob said, "I know we can work this out, but now I'm ready for a shower. I've got to go to work early tomorrow so I think it's about time to head to bed. Do you want to join me?"

Dane jumped up and followed Rob back to his room. After a very long shower, they finally made it to the bed.

CHAPTER EIGHTEEN

The next morning Dane woke up to the smell of coffee brewing. He was still in Rob's bed. He knew that they'd need to get dressed for work soon, but he felt like calling in sick just to stay in bed with Rob. Just thinking about the man, made him magically appear in the doorway holding two cups of coffee. Rob set the cups on the nightstand and said, "Sorry to wake you so early, but Marc is going to be here soon to pick me up for work. I thought you might want to be dressed and ready when he got here."

Dane was grateful that Rob considered that he might be uncomfortable having a stranger see them together. He only wished he'd been a better person back when they were in school. Rob and Dane took separate showers this morning because they each knew that if they got in at the same time, they'd both be late.

Rob made breakfast while Dane finished dressing, and then just before his driver arrived, Rob asked, "Do you care if Marc knows? He had to sign a confidentiality waiver before coming to work for me, but I do trust him. He's a good kid."

Dane deflected the questions by saying, "I need to question him about Jason and the phone calls. Just in case, to rule him out." He looked over at Rob and continued, "I know you trust him, but let's wait until after I've had a chance to talk to him first." He was happy when Rob dropped the subject and gave him a quick kiss on the cheek before grabbing his coat from a nearby closet.

Marc arrived a few minutes later, and Rob waved him in

81

from the front door. Rob ushered him into the kitchen where Dane was still seated drinking a cup of coffee. Rob started to introduce them when Dane stood up and said, "Hello, Marc. I'm Deputy Johnson. I need to ask you a few questions before you and Rob take off." He gestured to the other chair at the small table then turned to Rob. "We won't be long, but if Marc wants you here, you can stay."

He noticed Rob shoot Marc a questioning glance. When Marc smiled and waved to the last chair, he felt a twinge in his gut. He wanted to reach across the table and just pummel the life out of Marc. To calm himself, he searched his pockets for his pen and notepad, hoping Rob wouldn't notice his shaking hands. Luckily, Rob was too busy moving around the table.

As soon as Rob sat between Dane and Marc, Dane cleared his throat to begin the questioning, when Marc beat him to it. "Okay, what's up?"

Flipping open the notepad to a clean sheet of paper, Dane responded, "Mr. Owens has reported a case of harassing phone calls. We need to clear everyone who has access to his phone numbers as part of the investigation."

Marc's eyes widened and he glanced over at Rob. "You don't think I would do that do you, Rob?"

Dane noticed that Marc's hands were shaking and his breathing was starting to speed up before Rob spoke. "No, Marc. This is just routine. Besides, I'm pretty sure it isn't you since several of the calls came while you were driving me around."

Dane noted that the surprise on his face appeared genuine when Marc said, "Oh! The ones you kept saying were the wrong number?"

"Yes, Those ones."

Dane interrupted. "So you were there when he got some of the calls?"

Marc glanced over at Rob before answering. "Yeah, I guess. Sometimes he would get a phone call and then hang up right away. He told me they were wrong numbers, but I could see his face, and he looked scared a few times."

He looked over at Rob. "You didn't mention that he knew about the calls."

Rob said, "I wasn't really thinking about it. I didn't tell him they were harassing calls. I just blew them off at first. But, yes he was near me when a few of the calls came in."

Dane made a note and then turned back to Marc. "Okay, that helps us eliminate you, but Rob mentioned your old boyfriend yesterday. We need to run him as well as part of the investigation. What's his last name?"

Dane kept on questioning Marc until Rob laid a hand on his shoulder and said, "Dane, we need to leave or we'll be late. You can call him back or ask him later."

Dane noticed that Marc was watching them with interest. Finally, Marc stood and said, "If you're done for now, I'll go wait in the car." He flashed a grin and whispered in Rob's ear before walking out the door.

Dane watched him leave then turned back to Rob who was trying to stifle a laugh. "What did he say?"

Rob leaned over and kissed him before whispering in his ear. "He said that you're cute, and I'm a lucky dog."

Dane couldn't hold back the blush that crept up his face. He knew it would only be a matter of time before everyone knew, but he'd hoped it would be a while yet. He held Rob's hand as they walked out to his car. Rob would have a state police protection detail who would meet up with Rob at the studio. Dane wasn't worried about being caught here on Rob's huge property, so he stretched up and gave Rob a going away kiss and a promise to see him again in the evening.

***

Dane had trouble keeping the smile off his face all day at work as he followed up on Rob's case. He tried to tone it down after one of the guys on his shift joked that he looked like he'd just gotten laid. Then the rest of the crew tried to ask who the lucky lady was, but he found that he just wasn't as concerned about them finding out. Maybe soon he could tell them the name of the man who made him smile like that.

Late in the afternoon, Angela called to let him know that they had a breakthrough on Rob's cell phone records. They had been able to determine that one of the callers had made calls from his registered cell phone in California. She had contacted the

LAPD as soon as the information came in. LAPD picked the man up late in the morning and they'd just finished interviewing him. As soon as he got off the phone with her, he went straight to his boss's office to inform him of the developments.

He tapped on the wall beside the open door frame. When the sheriff looked up at him he said, "I've got a report on the Owen's case."

Rodriguez waved him in and said, "What is going on?"

"We have located one of the callers and the LAPD has him in custody. Problem is that he's not really our guy."

Rodriguez said, "What do you mean, not our guy?"

"Technically he didn't intend to harass Mr. Owens. Based on the information he gave during the interview, he met a woman at a bar, and she passed off Rob—Mr. Owen's cell phone number as her own. The man was trying to stalk her, but when he called, he got Mr. Owen's phone instead. Based on the California Penal Code, he's been arrested for attempted stalking even though it was a wrong number."

He felt the heat of a blush cross his face. He looked down at his notes and hoped his boss wouldn't notice his embarrassment. He never slipped up and called a victim by their first name. As he gathered his thoughts and went back over the notes, Rodriquez asked, "Is there anything else?"

He cleared his throat and shuffled through is notes for a moment before responding. "Yes, sir. The suspect's cell phone number doesn't show up on Mr. Owen's home phone records, but there are still three outstanding prepaid cell numbers from the Greater Los Angeles area that do. We are still tracing those numbers and trying to see if this suspect had purchased any prepaid phones, but I really think we are dealing with two different individuals. When they questioned the suspect, he knew Rob as an actor, but didn't even know that Rob had come to work in New Mexico. Apparently, this was all a case of mistaken identity." His face felt even hotter as he spoke. He couldn't keep slipping up like this.

"Sounds like a good start." Rodriguez looked over the notes on his desk and then continued, "I've checked the schedule. We have enough coverage that we can let you off this week to cover Mr. Owens while he's at home. There doesn't appear to be much of a threat since he's only received phone calls. He hasn't had strange packages or notes show up on his doorstep. The county commission is having a collective heart attack that we have such a famous person in our county and they didn't know about it. They've informed me that we need to make sure he's protected, because they don't want any negative publicity for the county. So it looks like you've been approved by the commissioners to make sure that doesn't happen."

He fumbled with his notes as he tried to put them back in order and mumbled a half-hearted, "Yes, sir." When he didn't hear a response from his boss, he looked up to find the man inspecting him intently. He swallowed hard before saying, "Will that be all, sir?"

Finally, Rodriguez shook his head and said, "Yes. If we need anything else, I'll let you know. Keep me up to date on the investigation."

"Yes, sir." Dane left the room still shaking a little.

Although they cleared one number off the list, that didn't help the investigation much. There were still several more unknown numbers to check out. Dane let Angela's team take the lead on the research as he wrote up the preliminary report on the case.

After he finished his shift at work, he went back to Rob's house to wait. Rob's hours at the studio were unpredictable, and he never came home at exactly the same time each day. This odd schedule made it harder for them to arrange a protection detail. As there hadn't been any physical threats or evidence of a stalker nearby, the adjoining agencies were reluctant to have one of their officers play babysitter for the actor for very long. Dane knew they needed to find the source of the calls soon, before Rob was left unprotected.

Throughout the week, Angela and the team continued to work on the phone calls from the unknown stalker. They found out that all of the prepaid phones had been bought at the same place in California, but they weren't able to trace the numbers back to anyone yet.

Every night Dane went back to Rob's house and slept wrapped up with his man. His man. He loved the thought of that. He really wanted to hear Rob call him that one day. Although they were getting along well, Dane was sure his feelings for the man were growing stronger by the day. He wanted more, but he was still so afraid of the consequences of coming out. He needed to wrap his head around all the conflicting emotions in him soon.

CHAPTER NINETEEN

Rob spent his weekend at home missing Dane who had to attend his weekend National Guard drill. Dane also had arranged for a substitute deputy for Rob's protection detail. His substitute deputy spent most of his time patrolling the perimeter of the homesite, checking through the barn and other outbuildings. Rob felt more alone, because he knew there was another person around who just didn't bother talking to him much.

Now that he had all this alone time, he realized how much he missed being with Dane. Even though Dane wasn't ready to tell the world about their relationship, he'd started coming out to his friends. The big reveal to Dane's parents wouldn't be easy.

Rob thought that making new friends with Dane and letting them come around while he and Dane were together might go a long way in helping Dane overcome his reluctance to show affection in public. Rob realized how isolated he'd become over the years. He didn't make friends easily. As he thought about the list he'd given Angela, he realized that only four people on that list had actually been to his house: Dane, Marc, and his godparents who used to live here. Granted his best friend Jess was halfway around the world right now, but she would come if she lived closer. Man he really needed to get out and meet some new people.

Rob knew that keeping Dane's secret safe for now was a priority. He needed to give his publicity team advanced notice so they could head off any speculation quickly. He called his agent to fill him in.

"Hey, Steve, I just wanted to let you know a few things. First on the harassing phone calls, they found out one guy was calling the wrong number. LAPD arrested him there in Los Angeles because he intended to call someone else. There are still phone calls from other numbers that they haven't tracked down yet. They want to keep this quiet for now. They aren't tying my name to the guy who called me by mistake, as he admitted that he was attempting to stalk someone else."

"I understand, Rob. I'll make sure to keep an eye on the news and not say anything about it. How's the show going?"

"Filming is going well. I hope this show stays around for quite a while. I love living here and working on a TV series. I also have a personal reason for staying around for a while. The second reason I called was to tell you that I'm seeing someone, but we want to keep our relationship a secret for now. I know I told you I wasn't seeing him, but the guy in the photo, that's who I'm dating."

"You're dating your bodyguard. Like Whitney Houston and Kevin Costner?" Steve laughed at his little joke.

"Ha-ha. Very funny, Steve, but yes, that's who I'm seeing. His name is Dane Johnson. He's a deputy sheriff and in the National Guard. He doesn't want to come out right now. If we're seen together right now, we're going to continue with the cover story that he's my bodyguard, but once that's over, we will tell people that we're old school friends who met again because of this stalker business."

"I understand. I hope he's better for you than Adam. That dude was—"

"Steve, just drop it about Adam. I don't want to think about him anymore. Dane's different. He's not interested in the fame and fortune. I think it actually scares him a little right now. Even if we were publicly a couple, he'd still be a little camera shy. Believe me, he's not like Adam."

After he finished talking to his agent, several new calls came in on his home phone. This time the messages were a little more specific. Someone apparently knew that he was in New Mexico. When the message started, he felt a sudden chill when he heard the distorted voice say, "Go home. We don't want you here. Leave before we make you."

He knew this time the caller was getting bolder. He hoped Dane and Angela would be able to figure out who was making the calls. He called the deputy in from his rounds and had him make a copy of the message for Angela's team.

After a long weekend with nothing but a few texts and short phone calls, Rob was looking forward to Monday night when he could finally be with Dane again.

Late Sunday afternoon, he received a text from Marc.

Can't pick you up in morning. At uncle's house branding and got kicked in head.

The reason Marc had come to New Mexico with him was so he could visit family, but he and Marc had never discussed what their families did. So Rob hadn't realized that Marc's family was into ranching.

Sorry to hear that. Hope you feel better soon. Is there anything I can do?

Marc's reply was almost immediate.

Not unless you're a dentist. Need to have some teeth replaced. Can't talk, jaw's swollen. Will let you know when I can come back to work.

Rob replied.

Don't worry about it, take all the time you need. Just get better.

Monday morning Rob decided to drive his godfather's old pickup truck that had been stored in the barn. Rob decided he didn't want to draw attention to himself. He figured that his Lexus SUV was a little too conspicuous on the local county back roads, and the old pickup truck would blend in better.

After a long day at work, Rob headed home. He stopped to get gas at a local convenience station and then headed out to his ranch. Once he turned off the main highway and headed to the ranch Rob had a weird feeling that something wasn't right. The traffic was always light on the back roads, but today, he noticed a couple of vehicles behind him. Occasionally he'd encountered other vehicles on this road, but it was rare to see more than one at a time. He kept an eye on the trucks behind him as he drove.

When he came to a steep, curvy section of the road, he slowed down. That prompted the first truck behind him to speed up and pass him. Rob's nerves heightened as he tried to keep track of both vehicles. Soon the two trucks had him boxed in, and he didn't have anywhere to go.

When they reached an area where the road widened, the truck behind moved as if to pass him. As soon as it drew even with his truck, the driver forced him off the road and into a muddy ditch.

His truck was still rolling to a stop in the deep clay mud, when the passenger in the other truck rushed to his door and smashed the window. Rob had just enough time to recognize the butt of a rifle in the man's hand before it came crashing down on his skull, knocking him unconscious.

***

As he regained consciousness, he first recognized the earthy scent of damp soil. As a breeze blew over him, the piney-vanilla scent of the ponderosa pine trees hit his nose first, followed by the scent of urine and feces. It was a far away scent that diminished as the breeze died down. He opened his eyes, but blackness surrounded him. He felt the moisture from the ground seeping into his clothing, and he shivered at the chills that ran over his body.

He tried to lift his head to look around, but a splitting pain in his head sent him crashing back to the ground. When he tried to cradle his head in his hands, he felt the stiff rope around his wrists and ankles. He was hogtied like calves at branding time with his hands tied to his ankles. He struggled against the ropes until he fell back exhausted from his efforts.

He didn't know how long he'd been out, but his throat was parched and his tongue was dry. He tried to call for help, but his voice was hoarse and scratchy. The earthen tomb he was imprisoned in dampened his cries. His wrists were raw, his head ached, and his muscles were stiff. Despite his discomfort, he closed his eyes and eventually fell asleep.

When he next woke up, a bright light shone in his eyes. Temporarily blinded by the sudden change from near total darkness to bright light, he couldn't see who was holding the flashlight.

The figure behind the flashlight squatted down beside Rob

and pressed a cool metal object against Rob's lips. Rob felt the drops of liquid as the person tipped up the metal container. The splash of water across his lips reminded him of his thirst and he drank greedily. Before he was finished, a noise in the distance had the stranger jumping up and pulling away the canteen. The light snapped off and they were plunged into darkness again.

Rob started, "Hey—"

But the stranger covered Rob's mouth with his hand and said, "Shhh." The deep voice suggested that his captor was a male. Soon the noises in the distance stopped. The man cut the rope that lead from his wrists to his ankles. His hands and feet were still bound, but now he could stretch out full length. Before he could ask anything more, the man slipped into the darkness and left him alone again.

CHAPTER TWENTY

Dane was excited to see Rob's Lexus in the driveway when he pulled up. He got out of his vehicle and ran to the front door. When he tried to open it, he realized that it was still locked. Rob never had the door locked when he was home, so why was it locked now? He walked around the back of the house to see if Rob was out on the back patio. Still nothing. Back door locked. Rob hadn't given him a key yet either so he couldn't go in and search for the man.

Dane walked all around the house looking for clues and checking the house for possible entry points. When he found none, he extended his search to the rest of the ranch outbuildings. Dane knew that Rob had more than one vehicle so he tried to figure out which one the man had used.

When he got to the old shed, Dane noticed the tire tracks where the old pickup truck usually sat. Rob rarely ever drove that truck because it'd been his godfather's vehicle, but it looked like he'd taken it to work today. He relaxed a little when he realized that Rob hadn't come home yet. Rob's schedule was unpredictable and he never came home at the same time, so he wasn't late yet.

Dane checked his watch again. It was now after nine in the evening. Rob had never been this late before. He started to get worried. He called Rob's cell phone and it went straight to voice mail. He sent text after text that went unanswered. He called Marc to find out if he had driven Rob. He wasn't able to get a hold of Marc as the calls all went straight to voice mail. Dane left a message asking Marc to call him as soon as possible.

Dane cursed, paced, and worried all night long looking for Rob. After midnight, he called Angela back in to help try and track Rob's cell phone. They were able to see that Rob had gone to Santa Fe and the cell had pinged a few cell towers on the way back home. The spotty coverage wouldn't let them pinpoint a good location. They got the general idea that Rob had tried to return. By five in the morning, Dane called his boss and explained the situation. They needed to initiate a search immediately. Sheriff Rodriguez ordered a search and rescue operation to begin searching for Rob.

He started calling the contact numbers on Rob's "safe" list. The director and staff at the studio would have been the last ones to see him so he started there. Then he called trying to get ahold of Rob's agent, but Steve's phone went straight to voice mail.

Steve called back later when he also couldn't get a hold of Rob's cell phone.

Angela called him around seven. She'd run a comparison of the cell phones that were still unknown. It appeared that someone purchased three phones at the same time in the same location. She'd already called the LAPD and they were checking out the store location the phones had been sold.

By nine on Tuesday morning, Dane realized that Marc hadn't come to pick up Rob, and put a BOLO out for him as well. He just started the search for Marc's home address when his phone rang.

"Dane, it's Angela. I've found some interesting things on the recordings. Apparently, some of the earliest recordings on the home phone were either erased or deleted, but there have been a large number of calls from a Daniel Baca."

"Danny is Rob's neighbor. Is his number on Rob's cell phone also?" That was interesting news since Rob hadn't once mentioned any of the neighbors calling him. But then again, Rob had kept most of the phone calls a secret anyway. He probably wouldn't have known about them if he hadn't heard that voice message the day he was over for the hike.

"No, it doesn't look like he called the cell number, but I think we need to check it out. I'm already headed that way."

"I'll meet you there. I grew up with Danny's kids. He can be a little rough around the edges." He hung up and headed out to his patrol car.

He caught up with Angela at the driveway to the Baca ranch, and they drove down the narrow, winding road to talk to Mr. Baca. Dane wasn't sure this was the right direction to be looking right now, especially with Rob now missing, but it was the only lead they had.

When Danny answered the door, Dane said, "Hello, Danny. We're here on official business. This is Angela Briggs from the state investigators office."

"What can I help you with, Dane?" the old man asked as he looked at the two of them.

Angela jumped right in, "Your neighbor, Rob Owens, has reported receiving persistent harassing phone calls, and we are just following up on leads. In checking his phone records, we found your phone number several times on Mr. Owens's phone records. Can you explain those calls?"

Danny was an old-fashioned man who didn't think women should be working outside the home, so he addressed his answer back to Dane. "Sure I've called the house. First I tried to get ahold of Carl." He turned to Angela as she was writing in her notebook. "That's Old Man Perkins. He used to own the place before he sold out to that actor." He turned back to Dane. "Anyway, since I knew he was in a bad way and had sold off most of his cattle, I wanted to see if he'd do me a lease on that land so I could run some extra cows on it. I never heard back from him. Later, I heard that Perkins had sold the place, so I wanted to try and make the same offer to the new owner. Didn't find out until after the fire that it was that actor."

"Have you been over on Mr. Owens's property since the fire?" Rob hadn't mentioned running into anyone on his property, but it didn't hurt to find out.

The old man scratched his head. "I was out checking on my cattle after they'd done that fire rehab. The fire crews had to cut the fence to get in. I wanted to make sure they'd fixed the fence proper, you know."

"Have you seen anything unusual in the area lately? Things like strangers hanging around, tire tracks, that sort of stuff?" Dane continued in his questioning. He was glad that Angela was taking all the notes because his own hands were shaking so hard, he was sure he'd never be able to write anything down.

Danny scrunched his face up in thought for a moment before he said, "Just seen that bulldozed area near the fire scar. Wanted to talk to Mr. Owens about that, but I've been busy with the fall round-up."

Crap, Dane had forgotten all about that strange disturbance. Rob was supposed to have called the Forestry office to see if it had been a part of their restoration after the fire. Dane hadn't followed up with it at all. He nodded as Danny talked about it.

"Yes, I know where you're talking about. We hiked past there on the way to Red Cliffs about a month ago. When were you last up there?" He wanted to know how recently Danny had been in that area.

"It was just last week. Rode the fence line while we were rounding up the herd. Gotta get the calves all branded and vaccinated before we haul them down to the winter pasture. Had to round 'em up early this year anyway 'cause of that fire. Forest Service says we gotta let the grass grow back 'fore I can put 'em back out there."

Just as they were about to leave, Dane noticed a man in the shadows walking through the back part of Danny's house. "Got company, Danny?" he asked casually.

Danny glanced behind him to the other man. "Just my nephew Marcus. He's back from LA. Got himself a job around here for the summer."

"Marc Glover?" Dane asked in surprise.

"Yeah, that's him. Have you met him?" Danny's expression of disgust let him know that the old man didn't approve of Marc.

Dane hesitated. Marc knew his secret, and Rob trusted him, but Danny was well known for his homophobic slurs. He finally spit out, "He drives for your neighbor, Rob Owens."

"That's the guy Marcus works for?" He turned and yelled, "Marcus. Come here."

Marc limped slowly into the living room. When he saw Dane, his eyes widened. Marc glanced over at his uncle quickly before looking away.

Danny spit out, "These guys tell me you're working for that actor who bought the Perkins place. That true?"

Marc nodded once quickly and then grabbed his head with one hand as he swayed on his feet. Dane noticed the large bruise and swelling on Marc's left jaw. "What happened to you, Marc?" he asked softly.

Marc tried to say something, the swelling in his jaw made it difficult for Dane to understand him.

Danny said, "Steer got him in the kisser the other day. Hell of a mess. How many teeth did ya lose, boy?"

Dane couldn't help notice how his hands were shaking as Marc held up three dirt-encrusted fingers as his eyes darted toward his uncle. Dane saw the fear and desperation crossing Marc's face. There was something more going on than Danny was letting on.

Danny continued, "Tried to have him help with the branding, but he's gotten a bit soft out there in the big city. Forgot how to tie up a leg and the steer kicked loose. Now I've got him working in the garden out back since Emma can't anymore."

Dane knew that Danny's wife Emma had had a stroke about a year ago. The paralysis was quite extensive and now she needed round-the-clock care.

Dane turned to Marc to see if he could get him to talk. "I tried calling you last night and this morning when Rob didn't come home from work. Did you get my messages?"

Marc shook his head slightly as if it pained him to move. Then he held both fists out in front of himself thumbs touching as if he was grasping an object. He twisted both fists quickly at a ninety-degree angle with his thumbs now facing up. Dane was puzzled for a moment until Angela spoke up. "It's broken?"

Marc nodded and gave her a thumbs-up sign. Then he pointed at his jaw and repeated the breaking motion. Dane got it now. "Your jaw is broken also?"

Marc gave another thumbs-up sign. His eyes kept darting back toward his uncle. Dane was pretty sure he wouldn't get any more information from them today, but he wanted to ask more questions. Just as he started to ask Marc something else, the dispatcher's voice came across his radio. "Deputy Johnson."

"Johnson here," he replied.

"Sheriff Rodriguez needs you to report to him on Forest Road 457 ASAP." He glanced at his watch and saw that it was now after ten. It would be almost eleven when they got there due to road conditions.

"Understood. Report to Sheriff Rodriguez on Forest Road 457. I'll be leaving the Baca ranch and en route. ETA thirty minutes."

He pulled out his wallet and slid out a couple business cards. He handed one over to Danny before moving to stand in front of Marc. He placed the card in Marc's front T-shirt pocket before stepping back. He addressed both of them when he said, "If you think of anything else, please give me a call." He looked directly at Marc and said, "If you need any help. You know where to find me."

Dane knew Marc had heard him when he saw the man twitch his hand out of sight of his uncle.

Even though Dane's gut was telling him something was wrong with what Danny had been telling him, he didn't have enough evidence to get a warrant. He wasn't even sure that Danny was intelligent enough for the sophisticated stalking that had been happening with Rob—the use of multiple prepaid cell phones from another state. There was no evidence to say that he'd made the harassing calls because they didn't have the recordings from Rob's machine. Without Rob to confirm, they couldn't even verify that Danny had called to ask about leasing the land.

The trip to the neighbor hadn't panned out like Dane had hoped, but there was still one more place to check out.

CHAPTER TWENTY-ONE

The darkness surrounded him again. Rob couldn't tell where he was or how to get out of here. The only thing he could do was crawl in the direction he'd heard the noises coming from. The noises had spooked his captor, so maybe that was good news for him. At first, he thought he'd try to stand up and hop along the wall, but he bumped his head on the low ceiling, and nearly passed out from the pain in his head. He rested for a while and slept again. He had no idea how long he'd been in this miserable hole and he wasn't sure if he would ever get out.

If he didn't do something, he'd regret it. He needed to get out and talk to Dane. He experimented with a bunny-hop-style crawl that helped him inch his way out of the darkness. With his hands and feet bound, he reached out with both arms and placed them out in front of himself. Then he hopped on his back end until his knees met his arms. He made good progress for a while, but he realized that he was crawling upslope. His hands and legs were shaking from the exertion and he had to concentrate on holding on while moving upward. Once, he slipped and almost rolled back down the slope, but he managed to catch a hold at the last minute. The ground grew rougher the further he traveled. He felt the sting of rocks scraping his hands and legs, but he still moved on. Surviving to find Dane was all he thought about as he moved.

He didn't know how long he'd crawled for, but he started to see a light ahead of him. He worried that his captor might be coming back until he realized that it was daylight he was seeing. If he didn't get out right away, at least now he'd be able to count days. It had been almost dark on Monday when the kidnapping happened. He had no clue how much time had passed while he had been in the total darkness, so he'd have to keep track from this point on. A noise ahead stopped him. Just because he saw the light, didn't mean he was going to rush out. There had been several men involved in his kidnapping. Some of them could be in front of him.

He needed a rest anyway. He wasn't sure when he'd last eaten, and he didn't know what day it was anymore. His hands were torn and bleeding from the rough ground. He found a spot near the wall that wasn't too rocky and settled down to wait. He still couldn't see anything except the light in the distance, but he could hear the noises more clearly. Despite his best efforts to stay awake, he drifted off to sleep again.

He woke up to the feel of cold hard steel against his wrists. He looked up to see a shadowy figure backlit by the bright opening. The steel blade cut the bonds at his wrist. As the figure moved to his feet, he finally recognized the man. "Marc—"

Marc's hand clamped over his mouth before he could finish. "Shhhh." It was the same voice as before when he'd been given the water. Marc looked toward the light as if searching for something or someone.

Rob couldn't believe that Marc would kidnap him. He'd helped the man and given him a job. Rob started to doubt his judge of character. First, Adam had betrayed him, and now Marc. What did that say about his relationship with Dane? Was Dane also playing him for a fool?

While he was lost in his thoughts, Marc resumed cutting the rope around his ankles. He'd never realized how numb they really were, but now the prickles and burning in his hands and feet told him the circulation was returning. Marc silently rubbed his feet and hands while keeping an eye on the lit area. Rob studied him for a moment and realized something was different. His face was bruised and swollen. When Rob opened his mouth to speak, a rough sound came out. Marc looked at him sharply, shook his head, then held one finger in front of his lips in the universal sign for quiet.

Once Marc finished rubbing the circulation back into Rob's hands and feet, he sat beside Rob and handed him a small water bottle. Rob drank quickly while Marc pulled a granola bar from his pocket and handed that over as well. Rob ate the food. It did little to curb the hunger he felt, but at least it was something. Rob changed his mind. Marc's actions suggested that he was trying to help. The man seemed to be on guard and intently listening for noises.

Rob started shivering as a breeze blew across his damp clothing. He hadn't been aware of it before, but now the breeze amplified the coolness in the tunnel, chilling him. When his teeth started chattering, Marc looked over at him then scooted closer to share his body heat.

Rob really wanted to know what was going on, but Marc wouldn't talk to him. Suddenly there was a loud crash and men yelling. He felt Marc tense when he heard a couple of men talking in Spanish. Rob had taken Spanish in school, but could only make out a few words. "Marcus," "hombre," and several choice cuss words.

Marc had done something to make these men angry and Rob could only guess what that was. The banging went on for a while and Marc remained on alert. Only when the noises died down and moved away did the man finally relax. It seemed their hiding place was still safe.

Marc seemed content to just sit there and wait. Apparently, he knew something, but he wasn't telling Rob anything. Rob curled up with his knees against his chest and wrapped his arms around his shins. Then he laid his head down on his knees and settled in to wait with Marc. He couldn't keep his eyes open and he slowly drifted off again.

CHAPTER TWENTY-TWO

As they headed to their vehicles, Angela said, "I'll follow you. I'm not sure where we're going." Dane nodded to indicate that he'd heard her, but his stomach was knotting up so bad he didn't dare speak. Forest Road 457 was one of the most dangerous roads in the area with its steep and rugged terrain and sharp drop-offs. Many years in a row, they'd had vehicle accidents out there. The mission to find Rob was top priority for the county. If the sheriff was calling him out to an accident there, it could only have something to do with Rob's disappearance.

When he arrived at the scene, there was a repelling crew preparing to go over the side of the cliff. His boss and other officers were looking at something down below.

As he walked up, his boss turned and said, "Just sending a team down now to check it out, but it kind of looks like Carl's old truck."

He thought his heart would stop beating at those words. No. This couldn't happen. Not now anyway. He'd just started thinking of a future together with Rob.

The minutes passed as the repelling team traversed the steep cliff and finally reached the vehicle. Dane nearly passed out from the waiting. His whole body was vibrating with fear and anticipation. He started to pace, but Angela caught his arm as he passed.

She whispered, "Calm down. You'll just make this whole thing worse if you break down right now."

He nodded because he couldn't speak. The lump in his throat was just too big. He swallowed hard trying to clear it away. He jumped when the radio crackled. "Team one to Command."

"Go team one," Rodriguez responded.

"Sir, it looks like Mr. Perkins's old truck, but we can't get into the cab to check for paperwork. I'll have to move around the back to check for a license plate. The outside is covered in mud, though. Looks like the red clay from further down the valley. Just wanted to let you know that there doesn't appear to be a body in this vehicle. As wrecked as it is, the interior is mostly clean. I don't see blood spatters that would indicate someone was in here when it went over the side."

"Understood. If we can hoist it back up, we'll need to send it to the lab for analysis. We don't know if the truck was stolen and dumped or if the owner was kidnapped."

Dane nearly cried with relief as he heard the exchange. Rob was still out there somewhere and he needed to find his man. Angela's touch on his arm brought him back to reality. He looked up and noticed his boss studying him. Just then, his phone vibrated. He looked and found a text from one of the unknown numbers they'd been researching. He grabbed Angela's arm as he opened the text.

Don't reply. Come to mine. Bring help. Take the right-most tunnel. M

Angela started, "What the hell? Do you actually understand this?"

Dane immediately contacted the Forest Service to find out the status of their rehab. He discovered that they had long finished and there had not been any disturbed ground or bulldozed sites when they'd left the area.

Dane's heart jumped. "I think so." He grabbed her arm and pulled her over to where his boss stood. He showed Rodriguez the text.

"This just came in from one of the numbers we've been trying to trace. I need to check out a site on Rob's property," he told his boss. "Danny mentioned it today and I've seen it before when Rob asked me to show him Red Cliffs. I don't know if it's important to the case, but my gut tells me something isn't right with that area."

"Tell me what resources you need and we'll get them out there," Rodriguez agreed. "The county commission is on my ass about his disappearance. They are all worried about him getting hurt on our watch."

His gut was telling him that was where Rob was located. It would take them almost an hour to hike in since there were no roads. If only he had a horse. Rob had been talking about getting a horse, but he wasn't home enough to take proper care of one. He looked at his boss and said, "We'll need horses or ATVs to get there. There isn't a road, and the trail is too narrow for a regular vehicle. The trees are thick in that area."

Rodriguez started, "I can call in the mounted search group—"

Dane stopped him. "No. This might be where the kidnappers are. If they have weapons, we don't need to put the civilians in danger. I think we need to send law enforcement. If there is anything up there, I think we will need the backup."

Rodriguez arranged for horses to be delivered to Rob's ranch, while Dane drove back to meet the team. By two thirty in the afternoon, the deputies arrived with their horses. Dane's nerves were shot. He needed to be moving right now, but the delays in arranging for the horses and men had stretched him to the breaking point.

He suppressed the urge to hop on the first horse saddled and race off to find the site. He knew they wouldn't be able to travel fast in the heavily wooded areas, and it would take them at least fifteen minutes to travel to the location. He nearly screamed when Sheriff Rodriguez ordered a quick safety briefing.

Finally, they were on their horses and moving. Dane was in the lead riding his aunt Liz's bay mare. In the open meadow near the house, he pushed the mare up to a gallop and let her fly across the ground. As they approached the wooded area, he slowed so everyone behind him could see the entrance to the trail. The steeper terrain and winding trail forced the party to slow down as they made their way forward.

It seemed like hours, but he knew they'd made good time when he spotted the first of the downed trees. He pulled the mare to a stop and waited for everyone to gather close. "I think we should leave the horses here and advance on foot. The open area isn't much farther. We can tie the horses to those trees."

He dismounted, led Liz's horse to a log, tied her to one of the branches, and waited until the others did the same. They approached quietly on foot until they found what appeared to be the entrance to a mine.

"Dane, do you know what's down there?" Rodriguez was looking through the binoculars at the entrance.

He struggled so hard to keep his voice steady as he replied, "No, sir. I've only hiked past the area once, over a month ago. I don't recall an entrance like that before, but we didn't stop the last time. We just hiked past here up to Red Cliffs and back."

"I see." Rodriguez started to turn around and address the deputies when two men walked out of the entrance. Their yelling could be heard from their position, but they couldn't make out specific words. They watched as the men dumped buckets of dirt into a large sifter and started shifting through the dirt.

Rodriguez turned to the men and whispered, "We need to set up a perimeter and see if we can quietly apprehend those two. We don't know if there is anyone else inside, so we need to be quiet about it." He continued to direct the deputies to their positions, then turned back to Dane. "Once they have the area secured, we and a few others will go inside and see if we can find your friend."

CHAPTER TWENTY-THREE

Rob felt Marc elbow him in the ribs and he heard the noises of the police as they went about checking out the cave. Rob heard them shouting at someone to drop their weapon and get down. He strained to hear Dane's voice, but he couldn't make it out. Marc stood and reached out his hands to help Rob to his feet. His legs felt like lead as he tried to walk with Marc's assistance. He'd lost all track of time, and was just grateful that Marc had helped him through this ordeal.

As they approached the main chamber of the mine, one of the officers spotted them. "Halt!" The deputy turned and said, "Johnson, is this who you are looking for?" Rob looked up to see Dane rush forward. He was stunned when Dane wrapped his arms around him and held him close.

"Oh god, Rob, are you okay?" Dane asked, before he stretched up and kissed him. He wasn't expecting that in front of others. Dane pulled his head down and pressed their foreheads together. He could feel Dane's hands shaking as they cradled his face. "I thought I'd lost you," Dane whispered.

Someone cleared his throat in the background. Dane stepped back, swiping a hand across his face as he turned to Marc, and said, "You have some explaining to do."

When Marc nodded, Dane turned to the other officer and said, "We'll need to take him in and get his statement. He's not a suspect at the moment. Treat him as a material witness." Dane turned back to Rob and said, "Let's get you out of here. Are you okay to walk?"

His voice sounded rusty to his ears as he said, "Yeah, I just need a little help. My feet are numb."

Dane took his hand and led him toward the entrance. Before they left the cave, the two officers met them at the entrance. As his eyes finally adjusted to the brightness, Rob recognized the men as Deputy Morales and Sheriff Rodriguez.

Rodriguez started. "I see you also have some explaining to do." As he looked down at Rob and Dane's entwined hands. "If you want this to be kept quiet, let Juan help him out to the horses. I'm not judging here, but some of the guys will have a field day with this." He paused. "I had a feeling something else was going on when the photo came out. I should have let you know then. This won't affect your job with me. I don't care who you sleep with as long as you do your duty as my deputy. If you want to wait for a while to tell the rest of them, that's fine. I'm probably going to order some sensitivity training anyway, because I know some of them might not like this. But I'll stand behind you if they make it an issue."

He felt Dane relax a little beside him. His heart jumped in his chest when Dane looked at him like a little lost puppy. He wanted to make that look go away so he squeezed Dane's hand and said, "I'll be okay, Dane. You go find out why they kidnapped me, and why Marc knew to help me. I'll be home waiting for you when you're done."

Dane's smile gave him hope that the man wouldn't let him down. He turned to Deputy Morales and said, "Good to see you again." He walked away with Juan toward the horses.

"You'll have to ride with me," Juan said as he mounted his horse. "We didn't have enough extra horses. They took the others down with the ATVs and quad runners."

Rob climbed up behind the man, and they headed out quietly down the hill. As they rode, he thought about how Dane had broken through his barriers for just a little bit and let his private self out. He knew how hard that had been for the man. He was touched that Dane had reached out like that. His doubts about Dane's intentions vanished with that simple contact. He knew Dane and Marc were both friends he could count on. Dane, though, was even more than a friend. The kiss Dane had given him in the cave had stolen his heart. He knew now that he and Dane were meant to be together. He just wished he could be sure Dane felt the same.

The Gator was waiting for them as they reached the open meadow. He fell when he tried to get off the horse. His legs just wouldn't support him anymore. He hadn't felt this weak in years. The deputy driving the Gator took him back to his house where an ambulance was waiting. He didn't want to go to the hospital and miss Dane's return, but his head was still hurting, and one of the EMTs mentioned the possibility of stitches.

CHAPTER TWENTY-FOUR

Dane and Rodriguez searched the rest of the small cave and tunnel system until they verified everything was all clear. When they inspected the sifting machine outside, they found small amounts of raw turquoise. Not much, but enough to make someone want to continue mining in the area.

They rode back to the house to find only Juan waiting for them. He needed to deliver the horses back to their owners' places. As Dane unsaddled his aunt's horse, Juan said, "Rob went to the hospital to get his head looked at. He'll probably be there a while. The EMT said he might need stitches. I told him to call me if he couldn't get a hold of you, and I'd go pick him up if you can't."

"Thanks, Juan. I really appreciate it. I don't know what all we still have to do, but we need to interview the suspects."

Dane and his boss loaded up their horses and watched Juan drive off. Then they followed and went to the station.

Dane found Marc first. Because of his broken jaw, he signed for a pen and paper. When he gave them to the man, he immediately started writing.

Dominic found the turquoise over a year ago, but had to hide the entrance for a while after the fires started. Dominic knew that his father wanted the land to run his cattle on, but Dominic wanted the turquoise. They paid the dozer operator to clear the trees around the opening after the fire rehab.

Reading over his shoulder, Dane stopped him. "Dominic Baca, Danny's son?"

Marc nodded and continued writing.

When I got kicked in the face, Dominic found out that I worked for Rob. I hadn't told them before who I worked for, but when Dominic found out, he wanted me to kidnap Rob. I wouldn't do it so Dominic beat me and broke my jaw. It wasn't broken from the steer kicking me. Dominic did that. He took my phone away and broke it so I couldn't warn Rob.

Dane had to keep his anger in check as he read that. He didn't like that Marc's beating was the result of him trying to help Rob.

I still refused so Dominic rounded up some of his friends who managed to get ahold of Rob. They kidnapped him off of the highway and took him up to the mine. When I followed them from Danny's house, they were holding him in the main area of the cave. While they were celebrating, I snuck in and moved him to that secret side tunnel. They didn't even know it was there. They were so busy drinking and joking around that they didn't see me move Rob.

I had to leave him to go back to Uncle Danny's house. That's when you found me there. I'd just come back from the mine. Danny didn't know what I'd done then. He found out after you left. He tried to lock me in one of the rooms, but I got out and found a cell phone. That's when I texted you to come to the mine. Uncle Danny and Dominic had planned the whole thing out. They were going to force Rob to sign over the deed and mineral rights to the property. I'm pretty sure they were going to kill him and make it look like an accident. I heard them say they wanted to drop him off the top of Red Cliffs.

Dominic talked his dad into it after they couldn't get Rob or Old Man Perkins to answer their calls. Dominic thought his dad deserved to own that land because it used to be in his family a long time ago. But they sold part of it to keep the rest going.

Dane noticed Marc's hands shaking as he wrote the last bit. He rested his hand on Marc's shoulder. "I think that's enough for now. Let me find you a ride home."

NO! Can't go home now. The whole family is backing Uncle Danny. I won't be welcome.

"Okay, we can find you some other place. Let me talk to Rob and Deputy Morales. We will find you a safe place to stay."

Dane rubbed Marc's shoulder to reassure him, then walked out to make his calls.

A couple hours later Dane was ready to call it a day. He'd been up over twenty-four hours by this point and was dead on his feet. Juan walked by and said, "I was going to go pick your friend up from the hospital. Want to ride along?"

He was grateful that Juan offered, because he didn't think he had enough energy to walk across the street to get a cup of coffee, much less drive all the way to Rob's house.

After escorting Marc out to the waiting vehicle, they all headed to the hospital to pick up Rob.

Juan dropped them all off at Rob's house, and Rob showed Marc to the guest room. Then, he and Rob made their way to Rob's bedroom. He held Rob close and whispered in his ear, "I love you, Rob."

EPILOGUE

One year later, Rob and Dane were back at their favorite spot. Crest Ridge was the place they'd made peace with each other, became friends and, eventually, lovers. This year at the cliffs, there had been rain, instead of fire. They played, well, skinny-dipped, under the waterfall for a time, before making love and falling asleep in the grass at the edge of the creek.

Rob woke up a short while later, pulled on his jeans, and leaned back against one of the many large boulders near the stream. As he watched Dane sleeping, he thought about all the changes that had happened over the past year. Rob took the role on the TV series so he didn't have to travel. The bonus that staying local gave him was the opportunity to get to know Dane better.

Dane told his family about his feelings for Rob and officially introduced Rob as his boyfriend. His aunt Elizabeth turned out to be the most supportive of his family, but Dane was surprised that his mom and dad hadn't turned him away. Now he could be Private Dane—as Rob called him—more often.

Public Dane still existed and had that don't-ask-don't-tell attitude when they went out in public. He was still coming to terms with himself and wasn't sure about outing himself to the world yet. When they went places, they introduced each other as old friends from high school. Every once in a while, though, Dane would do something that would surprise Rob. The other day they went to the little deli in town to pick up one of those famous green chili and pepperoni pizzas they both liked. For no apparent reason, right before they walked through the door, Dane grabbed Rob's hand for a second and smiled brightly up at him. Dane dropped Rob's hand almost immediately after, but at least it was a start on the public affection.

Rob watched as Dane finally woke up, ran his fingers through his already rumpled hair, and slipped into his jeans. Dane must have noticed he was being watched, and walked toward Rob. Before Rob could move, Dane blocked Rob in by putting his hands on the boulder on either side of Rob's body, then rose up on his tiptoes and gently kissed him.

"I love you, Rob. I'm glad you came back into my life."

"I love you too," Rob replied as he leaned down for another kiss. He remembered a year ago when he'd asked himself if it was worth getting to know Dane better, and he only had one response. *Yes, it was worth it.*

THE END

ABOUT THE AUTHOR

A cartographer by day, A. L. Boyd spends most of her free time with her horses, gardening, or reading. She never intended to be a writer, but stories like this one sometimes just pop into her head. The writing came about as a way to get the stories out.

CONTACT & MEDIA INFO:

Email: alboyd99@gmail.com
Goodreads: http://www.goodreads.com/user/show/16631303-a-l
Facebook: https://www.facebook.com/A.L.BOYD99

Also by the Author
Soaring Hearts - Contemporary Romance Novel set at the Albuquerque Balloon Fiesta.

Kickass Anthology - A short story in the anthology donated to help pay medical expenses for a fellow author.

The Dawn of Darkness - Contemporary short story written for the 2015 *Goodreads M/M Romance Group* writing event.